# Making a Hard Right

TURNS IN LOVE SERIES: BOOK TWO

THE CONSEQUENCES OF A WRONG TURN

## RENÉE A. MOSES

GUSSYFLO PUBLISHING

*To my great-grandmother, Gustavia. I'm doing this for us. I love you.*

*Momma, thank you for always believing in me even when I didn't. I hope you like this one.*
*To my Aunt Bridgette Gethers, you were my first reader so many years ago. If it wasn't for your support, no one would be reading my stories today. I can't thank you enough for giving me the confidence to become an author. I love you.*

MY STOMACH TURNED ON ME SINCE WE'D BEEN BACK from Central and South America. Out of the blue, I woke up sick. In Mexico, I was so nauseous it ruined the end of our trip. Well, for me it did.

When I first arrived in Muir Beach, I was antsy. Back home, I had a perfectly good career that kept me busy, and now nothing.

Moving here sounded marvelous in my mind. I planned to get over my relationship with Trent, my mom's constant "I'm so disappointed in you" breakdowns, and that one night of liquored-up dumb shit with Brian. I still couldn't believe I did that.

My cousins visited their mom with their families on my second night. It was a full house. Cory and Marissa had four kids, aged seven and below. Malik and Tara only had two. They were preparing for a move into a new home closer to my aunt and Cory.

Having the kids all together with their grandmother gave the exhausted parents a limited time to relax. I sat out on the balcony with the four of them while Aunt Vivica attempted to tame her grandchildren.

I learned that Marissa stayed at home with their four and Tara worked part-time at her boys' daycare. Since she worked with kids, she needed this quiet time more than anyone.

I got along great with children, but I had no desire to spend my entire days drowning in them. My nephews back home were angels for a few hours with me. But if I kept them all day, every day, I'd lose it.

My cousins lived decent lives with beautiful families. When they found out I recently broke off my engagement, the conversation took a turn. Married couples always wanted everyone else to tie the knot.

The question came up about my plans regarding marriage and kids. I told them I'd be ready when the right guy came along to change my mind about it all.

For now, being single and having no little humans depending on me was for the best. Trent put a sour taste in my mouth when it came to long-term relationships. I didn't trust my judgment with men anymore.

With the first week of this new start under my belt, I needed to figure out how I'd use my time here. My aunt assured me I didn't need all the answers right away, but something had to occupy my days. Since this was a break from everything, I had to learn how to chill out.

My aunt made me pick a book from her mini library. I never knew she loved to read. She had some of everything. In between reading, I binged on new shows I couldn't find time to invest in before.

Most of my TV experiences were with 90's sitcom reruns. They never got old and I didn't have to learn new people. Now, I was hooked on *Law & Order: SVU*, *Grey's Anatomy*, and *Power*.

Aunt Viv jogged in the mornings, and she usually ran on

the beach. The first time she woke me up to join her, I dreaded going out there.

Running didn't mesh well with my limited athletic abilities. My feet never quite landed on the ground securely. At least that's what I thought when I tried in the past.

My chest always burned when trying to catch my breath like something was wrong with me performing this activity. So, I usually avoided it altogether. Maybe it was in my head, but I hated it either way.

This time proved me wrong. I had a purpose behind each step. We started off slow and before I knew it; we raced against each other daily.

Aunt Vivica beat me in the beginning due to my rustiness. I became the champion by the fourth time. I didn't have a fitness motive. I ran from Trent. I ran from Brian and Denise. I ran toward my future.

After another two weeks, my aunt was ready to go somewhere, anywhere. Aunt Vivica didn't want to wait for me to settle in. She told me I had the rest of the year to do it.

Instead, she scheduled almost a straight month of traveling. How could I say no to that? My empty passport needed stamps in this lifetime.

ρρρ

WE BEGAN our journey to maximum relaxation. The first week, we visited Costa Rica and stayed at a resort off the beach called Occidental Papagayo. No kids allowed. Amen.

My aunt and I shared a room. She had the funds but wasn't crazy about wasting any of it. I preferred sharing the space. Auntie kept me occupied and distracted me from my thoughts. Her company was entertaining to say the least.

I never saw a place more beautiful. The blue ocean blew

my mind. I'd been accustomed to brown water shores in the Gulf of Mexico all my life.

The beaches appeared endless. The ocean breeze flowed through our room, peacefully waking us up each morning. True paradise.

Auntie showed me a lifestyle I would work my ass off to get one day on my own. This trip gave me a type of motivation I never had before.

This woman was an outdoors person unlike me. I enjoyed the beach but not hiking and long walks too close to nature. Surprisingly, the trails and tours changed my heart.

Some little creatures had me jumping all over the place. People thought I was crazy, so I tried to chill whenever I noticed any critters. In all, the hikes were fun.

Zip lining would also get a "hell no" any other time, but Aunt Vivica pushed me to let go and be free. I was glad I listened. This lady had me out there doing everything I'd swore I'd never do.

If anything changed me the most, it was the food. We ate the majority of our meals at the hotel, which was beyond delicious. A few times we ventured off and met the locals at nearby restaurants.

Southern cuisine was the only thing I found pleasing to my palette. Until I had no other choice but to immerse myself into the different culture and food. It opened my eyes to a whole new world.

Buenos Aires, Argentina, took the trip to another level. Alvear Palace Hotel provided a luxury I hadn't dreamed of experiencing. The place was straight out of a movie.

Hell, for a few moments, I thought I hit the lotto. The gold accented decor and marble everywhere in our suite made me feel unworthy. The elegant dining and even more beautiful city were the highlights of my existence.

Our vacation traveled downhill in Mexico. My stomach

had a mind of its own. The first thing I blamed was the food. I ate some of everything. Even though I enjoyed each bite, one of them turned on me.

I didn't have the energy to do any of the activities I was eager to take part of. Aunt Viv kept me company, stating she didn't want to leave me alone. So, we lounged around in proximity to a bathroom for the last week of our trip.

Once we got back to California, nothing cured this bug. Aunt Vivica prepared homemade soups, which tasted great but didn't stay down. I kept myself hydrated and chilled on the balcony for fresh air as much as possible. By nighttime, the nausea died down and gave me hope that it passed. The next morning, I was once again on my knees in front of the toilet.

Days passed with no urge to do anything outside the house. I feared public humiliation if I couldn't get to a bathroom. So, we rented movies and ordered takeout. Marissa planned to come over with the kids, but I didn't want to get them sick. She'd have to handle her herd alone for one more week.

After another day of lying around doing nothing, I improved a little. We thought the worst had gone, so we went bowling. I threw up there too. My aunt worried that it was something serious and wanted to take me to the hospital. With the help of the internet, I self-diagnosed my symptoms as dehydration.

When I was still sick after a week, my aunt asked if I could be pregnant. I laughed it off. Trent and I never had unprotected sex after my miscarriage. Having his baby would have been the nail in the coffin. I made sure not to get caught up in that type of situation.

The night with Brian came to mind. I didn't remember if we used a condom. There's no way we didn't. Does he even carry them?

The thought of him put me in the bathroom again. Life

wouldn't be so cruel. What we did was supposed to stay hidden. If I was pregnant, I'd have to move to South America and never return. No one would look for me there.

Aunt Vivica bought three different tests at the local drugstore. A half hour later, all three confirmed the end of me. We sat in my room in silence. My aunt wiped away many tears from my face, but they wouldn't stop falling.

The very reason for my relocation was to rid myself of the past, old and recent, and go a different route. This one was way off course. I didn't know how I'd turn my life around with a baby that belonged to a married man.

# *Kim*

"ARE YOU OKAY?" AUNT VIVICA ASKED CARESSING my shoulder.

All the tears had subsided after two days. My aunt kept inquiring about the same thing, and my answer hadn't changed since the first time.

Hell no I wasn't okay.

A kid was growing inside me. When my pregnancy was confirmed, my first thought was that I'd have to tell my mom and it terrified me. Of everything to be scared about, my mom's reaction sat high on the list.

"I can't believe this happened, Auntie. I can't have a baby."

"Mm, doesn't look like you have much of a choice now."

My head lowered onto the dining table where we sat. "I keep screwing up. It was supposed to be over when I came here."

"Hey, things like this happen. It's going to be okay. I know you wanted to be done with Trent, but it's impossible now that a child is involved."

I tried to clear my throat, but it itched suddenly. My

coughs were violent enough for her to get me some water. "Thank you," I said when she handed me the cold bottle.

"How are you going to tell him?" she asked after sitting back down.

"I don't have to."

Aunt Vivica's eyelids fluttered. "What do you mean?"

I didn't answer.

"Kim, don't be that woman. You can't deny your child's relationship with both parents. You will hate yourself for it when he or she gets older and asks questions. Plus, he has the right to know. You are better than that."

"No, it's not because of that...it's just..."

"What is it?" she almost yelled.

"It's not his," I spat out.

"Say that again."

I leaned back in the chair and fixed my eyes on the crystal chandelier above the table. "The baby isn't his."

Her eyes widened as she brought her hand to cover her opened mouth. "Oh my." She got up and poured herself a glass of wine. With my head back and eyes closed, tears flowed toward my ears.

Only one man could be the father, and there was no way he'd know about it. Telling him would blow up both our lives and the courage to do that was not in me. I would rather it had been Trent's baby. He's the less messy route.

Aunt Vivica returned with her glass and the bottle. I wished I could drink with her. I needed a tall glass more than ever. She exhaled, then tried to get more comfortable in her seat. "Tell me everything, Kimberly."

"I can't. It's embarrassing. No, it's sinfully shameful and will bring disgrace to our family."

"Stop being dramatic. Now, you screwed the man, didn't you? What's done is done." She handed me a paper towel to wipe my face.

"Oh, my God, Auntie."

"Don't use His name in vain."

"I'm not. I need Him on this one."

"Goodness! Is it that bad? You had a one-night stand or something? Don't tell me you don't know who the father is. Kim, no!" she theorized.

"I wish that were the case."

"Okay, now you're scaring me. Who is it?"

"It's Brian," I revealed, lowering my head.

Appearing to brood over what she had heard, she asked, "Brian who? The only one I know of is Denise's husband. So, who is *this* Brian?"

"The same one you know," I said, keeping my head down, avoiding eye contact.

Aunt Viv ran her hands through her short hair. She moved around in the chair and straightened her posture. "You mean to tell me that you are pregnant by the man who is married to your best friend?"

I nodded. The sound of the truth flowing from her lips made my stomach turn. Seconds later, I rushed to the bathroom gagging over the toilet until my stomach was empty.

When I cleaned myself up, we continued the conversation on her balcony. Even the view couldn't bring any comfort.

We sat for over an hour as I explained the entire ordeal with Brian back in college and our recent activity. The guilt weighed on me already, which was the main reason I moved out of Houston. The city wasn't big enough for the both of us. Instead, we created something larger than us and more sordid than the act that produced this baby.

What the hell was I going to do?

One thing for sure was that my parents could not know about this. Aunt Vivica thought I was insane to hide a pregnancy, let alone a baby. The plan was only temporary. Facing my mom now that we were in a better place than when I left was a no-go. If a miscarriage by someone I agreed to marry turned her away from me, then this pregnancy would make us permanently estranged.

ᛞᛞᛞ

I Skyped with my parents on Sunday afternoons, but by the sixth month, my face plumped a bit. I didn't look like a blimp, but it wasn't my regular slim face. Mom noticed and had to mention it. I convinced her we had been eating out so much and I worked out very little since moving here. It bought me some time until I'd drop the baby and the weight.

After another month, I lied about the app not working on my phone or laptop. The only forms of communication were calls and texts. No one tripped, so I was in the clear.

Daddy asked if I'd visit for the holidays. My due date was early November. Either way, Thanksgiving and Christmas would have to go on without me. So, I planned to say yes to the invitation, but I'd end up too sick to travel during my expected arrival. Nobody would force a sick person to travel.

Most of the pregnancy went well after the morning sickness ceased. Some days I cried like a baby knowing Brian and I made such a catastrophic mistake. My daughter, Ava, would grow up without her dad and that was on me.

I couldn't pray this one away. The consequences were too real, and I planned to deal with them alone. God knows I never meant for this to happen, but it's what I deserved for sleeping with Brian.

Other days, no one could wipe the excitement off of my face. When I felt my baby girl kicking, punching, and even hiccupping, it made the inexcusable truth of how she got here leave my mind. I loved her more than I ever knew I could love anyone or anything. Aunt Vivica talked to Ava every night. We read her baby books and sang to her.

I saw on social media that Denise had a baby girl and named her Layla. I missed my friend, but I couldn't get close to her again. That was on me. She'd be better off with better friends.

I didn't know what to call myself regarding us. My screw up took away my title of a friend. Instead, it was stalking on Facebook or Instagram, so I could see what she was up to. Seeing Brian in her pictures made it hard.

What have we done?

Life went on for everyone. Trent always had a picture of himself with different women in what looked like nightclubs or bars. It was typical since deep down I knew that was the life he wanted. I was happy for him to be free because it felt damn good for me too. Well, minus the swollen belly and all. At least I was free from his mess and only had my own to face.

Marissa, Tara, and Aunt Vivica threw me an intimate baby shower at the house. It was beautiful until I broke down in tears.

"What's the matter?" Marissa asked.

"I'm sorry. You guys, this is amazing. I only wish my parents and siblings could be here," I admitted.

"Aww, I know. It's sad that they couldn't make it," Aunt Vivica said.

We were the only ones who knew why. My cousins and their wives didn't know this pregnancy was a secret. It didn't matter because they rarely communicated with my side of the family. Not for any reason. Maybe the physical distance placed between us when we were all teenagers caused the disconnect. Either way, it worked in my favor ensuring that the beans wouldn't spill on accident.

"That sucks. Is there anything we can do to make it better? We can call them or make them a video or something," Tara suggested.

"No!" I yelled. "I mean, they are upset with me right now. We aren't talking."

"Mmm, that's unfortunate," Tara said.

"It's all good, though. You guys are more than enough. I can't believe you did all of this for me."

"Oh, please. You know I would not let your first pregnancy go on without showering you with gifts," Aunt Vivica said.

"Thanks, Auntie!"

"Now, wipe those tears so we can have a good time," Aunt Vivica demanded.

It was great hanging out with the ladies. They told me all of their worst stories being moms and provided enough advice to fill a book.

At the end of the night, the three of them walked me to the room next to my bedroom where Ava's nursery would be. We had done minimal work to it so far. I only recently decided on a forest theme. I imagined birds, foxes, and rabbits surrounded by trees.

Marissa opened the door to the soon-to-be nursery, and there it was. My forest on the walls. I bawled as I took slow steps around the room viewing every inch. The crib I told Aunt Vivica not to buy because of the hefty price tag stood in the middle of the room.

"You didn't!" I squealed.

"Looks like she did," Marissa stated.

"I know how hard this pregnancy and everything has been on you. I had to do something that would put that beautiful smile back on your face. You deserve it whether or not you believe it," Aunt Vivica explained.

The tears welled up so much that I had to pull my shirt up from my belly and wipe my eyes. The ladies thought it was funny. My aunt received the biggest hug I could give her with Ava between us. Tara handed me a tissue from the table in the hallway. I couldn't stop crying.

"How did you even do this without me knowing?"

"You didn't think all those spa days and maternity massages were excessive? I thought you'd catch on after the third time I made you go."

I laughed. "Not really. Carrying this load is doing a number on my feet and back. I thought you sent me out because of my complaints."

"Well, now you see what I was up to."

"You are truly the best."

I loved that I was joining the mommy club soon, but the remaining facts of it all took most of the joy away. The whole ordeal had to be a secret from the people I wanted to share these moments with the most. This whole "starting a new life" trip I was on when I moved here took a turn that played right into those words. Instead, I would bring new life into my screwed-up world. Ava deserved better, and I hoped one day when gets older, she could forgive me.

ϼϼϼ

MY PREGNANCY FELT like it lasted two freaking years with all the hiding and lying to my parents. The time had come to meet Ava. Boy, did she give me a hard time in the delivery room. I thought I could handle the pains of labor or what I imagined it would feel like.

My water didn't even break before the pain began. Hoping it was only a false alarm when Aunt Vivica insisted I call my doctor, he told me to get checked in at the hospital to verify whether the baby was coming. The drive took forever, but there wasn't any traffic since it was the middle of the night.

The nurse placed a strap around my belly that had a device that could monitor contractions. They weren't too bad, so I looked forward to going back home. After about twenty minutes, the nurse checked on me and asked if I felt anything. She explained that I was having many contractions between the ones I recognized. At that moment, I knew the delivery would be a breeze. I'd be one of the lucky ones who didn't experience major pains like the horror stories I'd heard.

Hours later, everything changed. I wanted drugs. Any kind. The tightening around my stomach grew stronger and came too often for me to care about being a soldier. I needed a hit of something. I screamed when I felt my bottom trying to run to the end of the bed.

Aunt Vivica called the nurse, and when she checked me, she rushed out and brought a table covered in blue cloth. It looked like the blue paper towels for paint spills. Then another nurse hurried into the room with tools that were unfamiliar to me. Another came in following my doctor with a bin that Ava would lie inside.

I placed my feet in stirrups, and they advised me to push. After letting everyone know I needed something to remedy the pain to keep going, my doctor said there was no time. Ava was crowning. Six hard pushes later, I heard her voice for the first time. I could fill a pool with the tears that fell once it was all over and they placed my baby girl onto my chest.

"She's gorgeous!" Aunt Vivica gushed.

"Yes...she is," I agreed through the short breaths.

I cried so hard; I couldn't breathe. This much joy and love was impossible until now. My baby girl finally rested in my arms.

# *Kim*

Ava hit her two-month mark. It was a mystery how I kept my baby from my parents. Every single time I talked to either one, I wanted to come clean but couldn't.

My dad was my heart, and he would love me through anything. If I told him, he'd have to let my mom know. That's when my nightmare would come true. The longer I waited, the more I wanted to hide out.

My baby girl turned a light on inside me. I had no idea it existed. Her coos and half smiles meant everything. I couldn't get enough of her. Aunt Vivica called me crazy for watching Ava sleep. "You need to get your rest too," she'd say.

It was so hard to break away from her because she was real. This little girl grew from a spec to a seven pounds three-ounce person in my womb, and I could touch her. For so many months, Ava could only hear our voices and now I heard hers. Nothing mattered more than every second I spent near my baby.

Regardless of how high on love I floated, my nightmares of Denise coming at me with a big ass knife were getting to me. It was more reason for us to keep this secret, throw it in a vault, then drop it into the ocean.

Aunt Vivica walked in on me staring at a blank TV screen and chuckled. "That show looks so interesting. What is it called?" she asked.

"Ha! It's called Death of a Homewrecker. Starring Kimberly Duncan."

"Ooh. That's depressing. Girl, stop acting like it's the end of the world. Everything will work out."

"How could it, Auntie? I can't get out of this one."

"No, you can't. But you can put your big woman panties on and face the laundry."

I turned and looked at her. "What? You said it all wrong."

"Oh, I know what I'm saying. See, you ain't no big girl. You're a big woman, and I'm not just talking about that donkey thang you sitting on since you had Ava."

My mouth damn near fell to the floor. Aunt Vivica cracked up at my expense. She knew I was sensitive about my baby weight.

"In all seriousness, that dirty laundry you are avoiding has to be cleaned sooner than later. I will always and forever be here for you, but that stench will get stronger. Eventually, you won't be able to live with it," she explained.

"Ugh, why?" I whined.

"Get yourself together. My brother will be heart- broken when he finds out, and now I'm an accomplice," she said.

"I know, I know."

"Make it right!" she insisted, walking away to answer the phone ringing in her bedroom.

I checked on Ava, who was asleep in her crib. My aunt made chicken salad this morning, so I went into the kitchen searching for the right bread to use for my sandwich. No one person needed this much bread. I only ate one kind, but Aunt Vivica damn near had a sandwich shop with this variety.

"Shit!" she whispered loud enough for me to hear. She rushed over from the other side of the great room between us.

"What is it?" My palms moistened. "What's wrong? What happened?"

Someone knocked on the door. Aunt Vivica jumped. "Ooh!"

"You're scaring me. What's going on?"

"Um, someone just called me and said to expect a package real soon. I didn't think it would be that fast."

"What?"

"Come with me to the door. It's for both of us," she told me.

"Uh, okay."

She gripped my hand, and it wasn't making this any less weird. I did as she requested and walked with her to the front door. She opened it.

"Baby girl!"

"H-Hey Da-Daddy." I felt my heart tighten as if my spirit was trying to bail on me. I hunched over for a few moments to catch my breath.

He dropped his bags and put his arms around me while I was still bent over. "Baby girl? Are you okay?"

I stood up. My aunt ran to the kitchen to get me a water bottle. "Yes, Daddy. I'm fine. You scared me."

"Scared? Now, why would you be afraid of me?"

"Aunt Vivica said it was a package," I said glancing her way. "I wasn't expecting to see you, that's all."

"Hmph. That was not at all how I thought you'd act when you saw me. It was supposed to be a big surprise."

"Oh, it was," I said inhaling deeply. I glowered at my aunt and her eyes widened.

"Uh-unh. Don't look at me like that. He called me seconds before he was at the door. I am just as surprised as you."

I held my chest while falling onto the couch. My dad went to the door and brought his things inside.

"Doesn't look like you're too happy to see me," Daddy said, sitting beside me. "Viv took over and wants to keep you all to herself, huh? Now you act like you don't know me."

We laughed and Aunt Vivica tried to defend me. Daddy cut her off. "Naw, you missed Thanksgiving because you were sick. Then Christmas because you two decided to travel. You could have come down to see us."

"My bad, I—"

Ava began crying. I shut my eyes hoping he didn't hear it. The way he whipped his neck toward our hall, he heard her.

"You got one of your grandkids here, Viv? I haven't seen any of them in person," he said, hopping from his seat.

Daddy was a fantastic grandfather. He loved babies and they loved him back. Some type of connection took place that would tickle the baby so much that he'd instantly become their favorite person.

"Um, yeah, that's uh my—" Aunt Vivica said.

"No. Don't," I interjected.

Daddy's eyes squinted before they bounced back and forth between Aunt Vivica and me. I didn't want to lie to his face. It was bad enough I lied about any of this. I regretted it all at that moment.

"What are you two up to? Have y'all been smoking again?" he asked my aunt while I walked to the nursery.

"That was years ago. You need to let that go," I heard her tell him.

The moment had come when I had to confess everything. I thought I had more time, but Daddy's poorly timed surprise clarified that it had run out. With Ava in my arms, I met them near the kitchen where they stood.

Daddy's smile beamed straight through my heart. The bliss he wore at the sight of a baby was priceless. He'd always say that babies were the most precious gifts God gave us. He said children gave their parents another chance to make a better life not only for the kids but for themselves.

I never understood how accurate it was until I became a mom. I wanted nothing but the best for her, and I knew I had to do better to give that to her.

The only problem with my perfect picture was one that could bring shame to my family and worse, to Ava. Hell, I hid my baby because of it. Not anymore, I guess.

"Oh, who is this little one?" he asked with the corners of his mouth almost to his ears.

We didn't answer.

"Which nephew does she belong to?" he asked, too distracted to notice me and Aunt Vivica lip talking.

She asked if I was going to tell him. I told her yes. When I hesitated, she waved her hand toward me to do it already. Daddy got lost in the baby. She was that beautiful. I could stare at her all day and had done it many times.

"So, I have something to tell you, Daddy." My dad smiled and talked to Ava while I held her. "Daddy!" I waved my hand in his face. He snapped out of it, then gave me his attention. "Daddy, this is Ava."

"Hi, Ava. What a pretty name for such a pretty baby. Yes, you are!"

I cleared my throat. "Ava is your granddaughter."

He paused and stepped back. Looking at me from head to toe, he put his hand on the back of his neck.

"Are you okay, brother?" Aunt Vivica asked, resting her hand on his shoulder.

"What did Kim say?" he whispered to her.

"This is my baby. Your granddaughter," I reiterated.

Daddy inhaled, and tears flowed down his cheeks as he exhaled. "Granddaughter?"

I moved closer and hugged him. Seeing him like this broke

my heart. It always occurred to me that things would happen this way, but it hurt worse than I imagined. My tears fell, and Aunt Vivica started soon afterward.

"I'm so sorry, Daddy."

"Sorry for what? You had a whole baby by yourself. I—"

"As opposed to having half a baby," Aunt Vivica blurted. His eyes darted toward her. "I couldn't help it. I hate when people say that. But she wasn't alone. We were here for her. I know we weren't her first choice, but she had us," she explained.

"How? When did you...I talked to you, and so did your mother. How did we not..." He took another deep breath.

"I hid it well. You had no reason to suspect anything, so it wasn't that hard."

"You were *pregnant*?" he asked, placing his hand on his forehead.

The baffled expression on his face had to be dealt with. So, I excused myself to breastfeed Ava. I cleaned her up and returned to the kitchen. They were out on the balcony but came inside when they noticed I was back.

I made Daddy wash his hands before I handed him his granddaughter. He cried again. Happy tears this time.

We sat in the living room as I explained everything to him. He didn't ask many questions. I told him about the delivery and how things had been since Ava was born.

"I cannot believe we missed everything. Your mom would have wanted to be here with you during your pregnancy."

Aunt Vivica and I looked at him sideways.

"Okay, well maybe not at first but no matter how disappointed she might have been, she would have come here for the birth," Daddy defended his wife.

I explained how Mom didn't make things like having a baby out of wedlock any easier. The whole miscarriage blow up was my first-hand experience of how unreasonable and judgmental she could be with my "mistakes".

Daddy reminded me he would not keep this from her and insisted that I told her right away. I agreed to do it after dinner. Then I could catch her right before bed. If she went off, I'd have an excuse to cut the verbal beating short.

We ordered from a Mexican restaurant and had our food delivered. Ava fell asleep before it arrived. Aunt Vivica put our selected entrees on the dining table, and we sat down to enjoy the first meal since Daddy knocked on the door hours earlier.

In the middle of eating, Daddy got a call from Mom. He let her know we were having dinner and that he'd call her right after. I knew it meant that I'd be the one making the call. I'd better enjoy my last moments having a mom that loved me.

"Kim?" Daddy said.

"Yes."

"Does Trent know he has a daughter here?" he asked.

"Whew!" Aunt Vivica said, coughing. "That bite was spicy."

"Do you need another water?" Dad asked her.

When I left that part out of the story, I prayed he'd be too overwhelmed that he had another grandkid to even think about how she got here. Dammit!

"I'll get it," I said.

"It's okay, Kim. I'm alright," she told us.

"You sure?" I asked.

"Mmhm." We looked at each other like a couple of kids about to get in trouble.

Daddy tilted his head to the side, narrowing his eyes. "Are you two playing around again, keeping secrets?"

"No, why?" Aunt Vivica asked.

"Because she didn't answer my original question and suddenly you got a cough." He looked into my eyes from across the table.

"Trent is not Ava's dad," I admitted.

"Then who is?"

"I can't tell you."

"Why? I know you know. You would not be that careless not to know. So, who is it?" he commanded.

I got lost in my thoughts, imagining how this would play out once I spoke that name. My dad had a heart attack in one scenario, screamed at me in another, and cursed me out in the last one. Not a single one played to my advantage.

"Big woman panties," Aunt Vivica sang.

"They don't fit. I can't do it," I responded, shaking my head.

"Y'all talking in code now?" Daddy asked.

"Sorry. Did you guys hear Ava? I need to check on her." I jumped to my feet and turned to walk away.

"Sit down, baby girl. Now!" I obeyed.

"I don't know what is going on here, but you are my daughter, and I love you with all my heart. You moved all the way to California, lied for a year by not telling me you were pregnant, and stole the precious moments from us to be here for you when you had your first child. I always supported you even when you and your mother went through many silent treatments, but I deserve better than this from you."

"Daddy, I know. It—"

"Let me finish, Kimberly. I am your father, and it was always my job to protect you until you found a husband to take over that responsibility. It's obvious that the father is not in the picture or you wouldn't be behaving this way. You had to have known him well enough to get into this situation... Unless someone hurt you. Is that why you won't tell me? Did someone hurt you and get you pregnant?"

"No! It's nothing like that. Look, I made a huge mistake being with someone and saying his name aloud is hard."

"Not saying it doesn't make it any less true," he pointed out.

I took a few deep breaths while both their eyes were on me. "Fine. It's Brian."

"Brian. Okay, does he have a last name? How did you meet him?" he asked.

"Daddy, it's Brian from back home," I clarified, looking down at my plate.

"*Brian, Brian*? Denise's *husband*, Brian?"

"That's what I said too," Aunt Vivica added.

I closed my eyes, wishing all of this could go away.

"Oh, baby girl," he said with the heaviest tone of disappointment.

As the tears fell from my eyes, I excused myself from the table and went to my room. Nothing was worse than hearing my dad's displeasure.

What else did I expect?

*Kim*

The next morning, Daddy got up before we did and prepared breakfast. I loved it when he cooked. His specialties were barbeque and breakfast.

When we were kids, Saturdays were the absolute best. We'd wake up to a nice spread that Daddy put together. It was his way of giving Mom a break.

He made pecan waffles, which I'd never turn down, depressed or not. I put Ava in a swing on the low setting next to the dining table. He would watch her and tear up.

Daddy kept complimenting Ava's beauty, saying she looked like me at that age. I prayed many nights that she'd favor me more. No one would care who her dad was if she didn't resemble anyone but her mother.

"Baby girl, we have to call your mother today. I'd rather we do it early in the day because of the time difference."

"Okay, Daddy."

Aunt Vivica said she'd be leaving to visit her sons to give us some privacy. She wouldn't want to be in the same house once my mom got wind of what we had been hiding.

Mom was a little jealous of my relationship with my aunt,

and she had no one else to blame but herself. Aunt Vivica having my back in this mess was proof of how close we were, and I trusted her with everything.

I asked my dad to give me a few minutes after breakfast to get myself together. Coming clean to my mom was as bad as facing Brian.

My aunt and I cleared off the table. We washed the dishes together while Daddy took Ava in the nursery.

"Auntie, I can't do this. It's too much," I whined.

"Girl, who you telling? You got yourself into this craziness. You have no choice but to deal with it. You can't hide Ava forever."

"I had every intention on coming to my parents on my terms."

"Well, hey, maybe God needed to give you a push. Otherwise, you would have kept delaying the inevitable. Besides, you're overthinking it. You act like Diana is a judge that can sentence you to death or something. You are human. You did a human thing, and she gets a granddaughter out of it. Once she sees Ava, whatever bad thoughts she may have will fly out the window."

"I hear you, but you don't know my mom. She can be so brutal when I do something she is against."

"Really?"

"Yes. She called me all kinds of whores when I was a teen. If I stayed out too late, she accused me of sleeping around with some boy. And I was only with my girlfriends back then. I was still a virgin years after that. Nothing I did was good enough when she had made it up in her mind I was in the wrong even when I wasn't. I hated it."

"That's tough. Your mom probably worried you'd get knocked up or something like she did."

"Well, at least she got married beforehand. That's the only way pregnancy is accepted in her eyes."

Aunt Vivica burst out laughing. "Is that what she told you? Wow!"

"What are you talking about?"

"So, since it's supposedly a secret, don't tell her you heard it from me. Kim, your parents got married when she was pregnant with you."

"You a freaking lie."

"No, yo' momma is." We laughed.

"Are you kidding me? She gave me such a hard time. She made me feel like the unworthy heathen of the family for the things I've done. You mean to tell me she has been lying all my life."

"Okay, don't get dramatic. It sounds like she wanted you guys to do better than they did. It was a struggle. Your grandmother damn near disowned her until she married my brother. It's not like they didn't love each other. Your dad just wanted to be in a better position in life before gaining a wife. Once he got on his feet with a good job and was able to take care of your brother and mom, he married her."

"Man, she acted like they fell in love at first sight and got married soon after. I don't believe it."

"You are a lot like her. Strong-willed, hard- headed, and as stubborn as a mule when you want to be. Lying so you won't seem so bad. That has Diana written all over it. Her ways may differ, but you two are the same."

"No, we are not."

"See?"

I splashed her with the water I used to rinse the dishes.

"All I'm saying is that she wants the best for you and she is hard on you so you'd want the same. She will not be the monster you claim she is with this one. She will have no choice but to understand. Ava is already here," she explained.

"Well, when you put it like that, I guess it won't be that bad. She'd probably kill me. That's all."

"Oh, stop it. You are a grown woman. Once you start acting like one, she will respect you as one."

"What do you think I've been doing?"

"Let's see, um, lying about anything personal, hiding your pregnancy, keeping the news that she has a granddaughter from her. Shall I go on?"

I rolled my eyes. "Ugh, no. I see where you're going. I am the one giving her the ammo by not confronting her."

"Right. It's not like you have to tell your mother everything. Again, you are a grown woman, but you shouldn't ever have to hide and keep secrets. She loves you, and no matter how hard her shell is, it will crack sooner if you be straight up with her from the beginning. Unless you want to be like her and your grandmother."

"Ooh. Good point. I don't want that at all. Dang, is that what I've been doing?"

"You moved all the way here because you didn't want to face her after you disappointed her."

"Well, that wasn't the only reason."

"True. But you still ran and running is a sign of immaturity and weakness. Now if you would've faced her on your terms and talked to her, even if she acted like she didn't listen, you wouldn't be afraid of her."

"I am not afraid of her." Aunt Vivica looked at me sideways. "Okay, fine. You don't understand how hard it is to be human and still stay in her good graces. That face she makes and her tone is so cold."

"So, what? You need to stand up for yourself. She is your mother, not Jesus. Her disapproval should not dictate your life."

I couldn't fight her on that one. I had been so focused on keeping my mom happy by saying what she wanted me to. It was time to be the grown woman I claimed to be.

We finished cleaning the kitchen, and she got ready to

leave the house. On the way out she told me to be strong and take responsibility for my life without trying to explain my actions. I'd at least try.

My dad thought it would be best if I Skyped with mom first and tell her about Ava. Then he'd come into frame holding my baby. I followed his directions, and we made the call.

Mom's smile made this so much harder to do. In my head, Aunt Vivica said, "big woman panties."

After small talk, I grabbed a photo of me while pregnant and held it up to the camera.

"What is that?" Mom asked.

"That's me, a few months ago," I shared.

"Um, no because that person looks pregnant. I noticed you gained weight, but you could not have gotten that big. Look at the stomach," she pointed out.

"Mom, please don't be mad at me."

"Kim, what are you saying?"

"I'm saying...that I...had a baby," I confessed.

"No, you didn't. There is no way."

"Yes, I did. I have a daughter now."

She stood up and walked away from the screen for a few moments.

"Mom," I called out.

"Put your dad on. I can't...this isn't real. Just put Dad on," she commanded off-camera.

Daddy was nearby and heard her, so he walked over and sat next to me with Ava cradled in his arms. "Hey, Honey."

"Harold, what is going on?" she asked still out of view.

"Sweetheart, I can't see you. Look at me," he requested. Mom sat back down in front of the camera. "This is our granddaughter, Ava."

"Oh, God! No, no, no," she yelled. When she cried, I did the same. "Why would you do this, Kim?"

"Mom, I can't change—"

"No, I'm not doing this right now. I'm not," she said before the call dropped and the home screen returned.

"That went well, don't you think?" Daddy joked, getting up from his seat.

"She never even looked at Ava. I told you she'd hate me as soon as she found out."

"Don't worry, baby girl. I will talk to her."

"Why is she so mean? It's a lot, but why can't she be mature for once and stop shutting me out every time I try to face her."

"It's her process. Kimberly, this is not a simple thing to spring on anyone. You had a baby without our knowledge. It's heartbreaking that our daughter kept us in the dark. I'm still trying to wrap my head around it."

"I cannot apologize enough for it, but I didn't think I had any other choice."

"You had a much better choice, and you didn't make it. This one is not on your mother. You dropped a bomb on us. The aftermath is not up to you. We love you, and not even this will change that. Your mom may need time to come around. You know how sensitive she is."

As much as I wanted her to be happy for me the second I told her, my mom had every right to be upset. It was a lot to ask of her. Ava was here, but I had plenty of time beforehand to say something. I understood her frustration with me and would wait for her to be okay with at least seeing her grand-daughter the next time we'd video chat.

Daddy and I got Ava cleaned up together. He only handed me the wipes and diaper, but it was nice to have one of my parents involved. We took a walk at a nearby park with the stroller and talked. I also told him about what Aunt Vivica said about Mom having my brother before they got married.

He couldn't comprehend why his sister didn't keep her

mouth shut about that but kept my secret from them. Favoritism was to blame in his mind. Daddy joked that Aunt Vivica loved me more than she did him or my mom.

Aunt Vivica was gone for hours and missed the lunch Daddy made. We had the best BLT's I'd ever eaten. Maybe it was because my dad wasn't judging me in all this. He was still just Dad. I needed that more than ever.

We were in the living room playing on a floor mat with Ava when I got a call from Mom. She looked like she'd been crying. After a few words, she asked if she could see Ava. I agreed and picked her up so she'd be in the camera's view. I answered with my phone, so Daddy grabbed it for me to hold it in front of all three of us.

Mom had tissues in her hand and kept wiping her eyes. "What's her full name?"

"Ava Briana Duncan."

"That's beautiful," she said, smiling through her never-ending tears.

"Thank you."

"Kim, I don't know what to say right now. I am hurt that...I'm hurt that you didn't tell me. I love you, but I need a little more time, okay?"

"Of course, Mom. I am so sorry I made things this way. Please forgive me," I pleaded.

"I will talk with you all tomorrow, okay?" she said, sniffling.

"Okay, honey," Daddy replied.

"Bye, Mom."

She waved and hung up. The mountain on my shoulders lifted. I sank into the couch feeling a little accomplished.

My dad frowned. I could tell he wanted to say something and if he was holding it back, something had to be wrong.

"What is it, Daddy?"

"You named her after him, huh?"

"Oh, you caught that."

"I did. So, let me ask you this. When do you plan on telling Brian he has a daughter with you?"

I lay my head back on the couch. No answer came to mind that would please my dad. It was clear what he wanted me to say, but it wouldn't be the truth.

"Baby girl, you cannot do this on your own."

I crossed my arms over my chest. "Why not?"

"Okay, you shouldn't do this on your own. This child didn't get here that way."

He played with Ava while lecturing me. Every now and again he'd glance my way. I had nothing to say.

"I get the embarrassment of it all, but you and that married man chose to lie with one another."

"Daddy, I don't want to talk about this." I turned away from him.

"Kimberly, look at me. You and Brian created this predicament. Facing him is the right thing to do. Your actions had consequences. You can't run and hide. Ava has a right to have a relationship with her father and vice versa."

"It's not that easy."

"No one said it is. What you two did was awful, but keeping Ava from him will be a price she'd pay for down the road, and she did nothing wrong. You did."

"I know! I know. She does deserve a relationship with her father, but Daddy I can't. It's messy enough and will ruin everything for him and Denise. I refuse to screw anything else up. Ava will be fine with only me."

"Now, you know that isn't true."

"Yes, it is. I will be enough for her, and when she asks about her dad, I'll tell her he died soon after she was born."

"Oh, so you have it all figured out?"

"I do."

Aunt Vivica unlocked the garage door and walked inside.

Daddy dropped the subject, and I took Ava to nurse her and put her to bed.

I showered and joined them on the balcony. My aunt poured me a glass of wine. The moment I took my first sip, I had to listen to them double team me about telling Brian. It wasn't like I didn't agree with their points. The fallout of it would be too much. I didn't find it worth it.

I respectfully asked my dad to drop it for the night. He agreed but made me promise not to tell my daughter her father was dead.

Ava needed love to have a great life, and she'd have plenty of it. She had my family. Soon enough, everyone would have to respect my wishes or stay away from my daughter and me.

# CHAPTER
# FIVE

DADDY STAYED FOR ANOTHER THREE DAYS BEFORE heading back home. We made the most of his time here, and he bonded well with Ava. I showed him every picture of my pregnancy and the video of us after she was born. My poor dad cried as much as my newborn in the video.

He selected many photos to take. We ordered prints online and shipped them to my parents' house. Plus, what seemed like hundreds of pictures he took with Ava during his visit. She was the first granddaughter and would be completely spoiled.

Mom begged my brother and sister to give her a grand-daughter. Her prayers were answered through her harlot of a daughter. When she and Ava meet in person, my mom would be more grateful than ashamed.

We had a civil conversation about how hurt she felt when she found out. Accepting she couldn't change it, she would not hold it over my head. If she followed through with that, it would be the biggest miracle of my lifetime. Judgmental was her middle name, and her full name followed right behind its definition in the dictionary. We would have to wait and see.

My cousins and their wives came over for dinner for my

dad's last night, and he got to meet Aunt Vivica's army of grandkids. With only two sons, she had six grandchildren, and more were in the works. Tara made it clear that she wanted at least four.

The guys talked about sports and playing golf. My dad's two favorite topics on the planet. He hadn't seen my cousins in many years and promised it wouldn't take as long for his next trip to Cali.

The morning before his flight, he tried again to convince me to talk to Brian. Daddy needed to get over that one. I made my aunt and dad promise to keep this between us until I felt comfortable enough to share the details of Ava's father with anyone else. Mom would have to be in the dark for a while longer. Brian would die in the dark.

We celebrated Ava's third month with professional pictures and cupcakes for me and Aunt Vivica. She said she did the same with her boys when they were babies. I liked the idea since I got custom desserts out of it.

My parents even called to talk to her as if she could understand anything they said. It felt good to have her grandparents connect with her.

ᛉᛉᛉ

EVERY DAY AUNT Viv gave me an hour off no matter what. Usually, Ava was awake in the afternoon. So, my aunt would watch her so I'd have some time to myself to do whatever. Most of the time I snuggled with a Black Romance book. It was my only access to a loving relationship. I had to get my fix from fictional love to hold me over until the day I'd find it for myself.

After finishing the book I started last week, I wrote my review on Amazon. Marissa knew an author and stressed to me how important reviews were. Since then, I always wrote my review immediately after reading.

With a little less than a half hour left of my break, I surfed the TV channels. I got bored quickly and searched for another book to start instead. Books were a better escape anyway.

An unknown number called me. It had a Houston area code, but I didn't recognize it. After the third call, I ignored it and texted them.

**Me: Stop calling. You have the wrong number.**

**Unknown caller: This isn't Kim?**

**Me: Who is this?**

**Unknown caller: Brian.**

I dropped the phone and stepped away. Every breath I took became harder than the last. What did he want? How did he even get my number? I changed it when I moved.

Aunt Vivica played with Ava in the nursery. I wanted to tell her, but she opposed my view regarding him, and wouldn't make this any better.

After a few deep breaths and hoping my heart would take the hint to slow down, I picked up the phone.

**Me: How did you get this number?**

**Brian: I ran into your dad. He gave it to me.**

My heart descended to my stomach. My dad sold me out? No words came to mind. Brian found out about Ava.

I plopped down on the floor since walking a few feet to the sofa seemed infeasible. My legs refused to work with me. Maybe they feared the dreadful possibility too. Another text came.

**Brian: I realize this is out of the blue, and I am not trying to go against our agreement to stay away from each other. But when I saw your dad, I figured it must be a sign.**

**Me: What are you talking about?**

**Brian: Answer your phone. I'm about to call.**

He did, but I let it ring a few times contemplating on ignoring it. Once I answered, he talked about Denise only. He didn't mention Ava. My body released most of its tension.

Brian asked if I'd visit Denise since she suffered from post-partum depression. Apparently, Denise refused to get treatment for the first two months after she gave birth to Layla. He thought something seemed off about her, but Denise dismissed it until her doctor diagnosed her with PPD.

She improved gradually with therapy. However, she mentioned my name a lot and expressed her anger about me leaving the way I did. Brian assumed that if I visited her, she'd get better sooner.

"Have you lost your mind?" I asked.

"I know it's a lot to ask of you, but I'm desperate."

"Things are too far gone for me to come back."

"Kim, you were her closest friend. You left her behind without even saying goodbye."

"You know the reason why I couldn't."

"Please. I am begging you. I will go out of town or whatever when you are here, so we don't have to be around each other if that's what you want. Denise misses you, and I can't fix it any other way."

"Can I write her a letter or send her a postcard or something? I am not coming there."

Brian exhaled into the phone. I sympathized with what she went through, but his request required more courage than I possessed.

"Kim! Kim! Your daughter is in here trying to roll over already!" Aunt Vivica yelled from the hallway.

"Whoa! Who's that? What did she say?" he asked.

"Nobody. Nothing. Look, I have to go."

"Kim, wait. Someone just said your daughter?"

"Um, no. That was...my TV is on too high."

"No, it sounded like—"

"So, I will write that letter okay. Bye!" I hung up. He called back a couple times, so I turned my phone off. Dammit, Aunt Viv.

ᗷᗷᗷ

DENISE and I chatted over text for about a month. When she asked why we never talked on the phone, I told her I needed more time. I used my breakup with Trent as an excuse for me not being over her and Brian's involvement. She bought it enough to keep this going for this long.

I enjoyed talking to her again, but then I'd look at Ava, and that mountain of guilt reappeared. Denise sent me pictures of Layla who was so beautiful and looked too much like Ava.

Everything reminded me of that one night. Whenever I saw her name across my screen's notification bar, I'd cringe. I imagined that one of these days she'd ask me about my daughter. She had no idea, but damn I was paranoid about her confronting me.

Aunt Vivica and I booked a flight to Houston for next week. My mom refused to wait any longer to meet her granddaughter. I promised we'd come out for two weeks.

Mom didn't visit when Daddy came because of a sudden severe cold. Knowing my mom, she lied. She had a fear of flying, and my dad hated road trips more than a few hours long. We didn't get to go too far from home during childhood because of their crazy combination.

Ava had a four-month checkup this afternoon. Marissa swore I'd love the pediatric clinic she took her kids to. It was almost an hour away from Aunt Vivica's house.

While in Richmond, I planned to visit Marissa. Ava's big cousins loved to play with her. Babies brought out the curiosity of younger kids. They never related to being so small.

Our original pediatrician left the office due to a move, but she referred me to her colleague in the building. We'd meet Dr. Thomas for the first time today. The long drive gave Ava a chance to nap, so she perked up upon arrival. We signed in and waited for a nurse to call us. There were only a few others in the waiting area.

One lady asked me if I cared about her breastfeeding her newborn. We made small talk while she did. The woman described two occasions when someone spoke to her about her feeding her child in public. It's not like she popped it out. She used a cover. I explained that some people were simply ignorant and insensitive. Babies needed to eat too.

A young nurse called us to the back and started the checkup. Everything looked good, and I had no real concerns to bring up. I never traveled with a baby before, so I wanted to see if a plane ride would be okay. She eased my worries but would mention it to Dr. Thomas. We waited in the room for less than five minutes before the doctor entered.

"Hello, there! You must be Mrs. Duncan," he said.

"Miss, but yes."

The doctor sat down in his chair. "I'm Dr. Evan Thomas. It's very nice to meet you."

I smiled and said nothing. Something stupid was bound to come out. He made me nervous.

"Hi, Miss Ava. How are you today?" he asked.

Ava cooed and smiled. I did the same on the inside. Dr. Thomas was fine as I don't know who, what, or why. My eyes had to stay on my baby girl so I would avoid his.

When did they make pediatricians like this? I thought they were mostly women and if a man's name popped up, he'd be old as dirt. Dr. Thomas could examine me anytime.

I had to stop my mind before it traveled too far into the gutter. This was about Ava, and I had enough trouble dealing with men in my life. But, dayum!

Dr. Thomas asked me about my concerns with traveling. I

gave him the short version so he wouldn't have to say too much. It didn't work. The man's voice was smooth and deep. He stood at least six-foot-two and was heavenly built from what I could tell through that white jacket.

After giving me some tips, he asked if I had any additional questions. The only ones that popped in my head had nothing to do with Ava's health, so I kept them to myself. He ain't got no right looking like that in this clinic. I rushed out of there. It had been too long since I'd been with anyone, and I knew better to even want to.

I drove over to Cory and Marissa's place. She had never met Dr. Thomas. I told her he looked so good I thought someone set it up as a prank.

Marissa had the baby swing ready for me. I laid Ava in it while we sat at the kitchen table eating cheesecake.

"I have Dr. Silverman, and his name describes him perfectly. He's a silver-haired old man."

We laughed. "That's who I should have gotten. Ava's doctor was overloading my senses in an inappropriate way."

"You are crazy! But is he really that good looking?"

"Girl. He's so fine I may need to find another doctor. I ain't got time to be seeing all that chocolate goodness every time my baby needs her checkups."

"Well, ask him out."

"The hell. I don't ask men out."

"Why not?"

"That's not how I roll. Besides, I have Ava. I'm not ready to be involved with anyone right now."

"Are you still in love with her father?"

I stopped eating. No one had ever asked me that before. I never asked myself that question. It didn't matter either way. Brian was off-limits, and I wished we both would have respected that fact a year ago.

"No. What happened between Ava's dad and me wasn't love. It was only one time. That was all it took, I guess."

"Oh, I'm sorry. I shouldn't have asked. It wasn't my business."

"It's okay. I need to talk about it. Like my family says, 'not talking about it doesn't make it any less true.' So, it's all good."

We headed back a couple hours later. I had to get home for my scheduled video chat with my parents.

OUR FLIGHT LANDED IN HOUSTON, and my dad came inside the airport to help us get our bags. I expected my mom to be with him, but he said she had to finish up cooking dinner.

We pulled into the driveway, and I noticed my brother's car parked there. My siblings found out about Ava when Daddy was in California. Everyone was shocked and assumed my baby was Trent's. I lied and told them it was a one-night stand and that the father wouldn't be in her life.

Aunt Vivica opened the door to the house. "Surprise!" everyone yelled.

The living room was decorated with pink balloons and streamers. A banner read "Welcome home, Kim and Ava!" There was a table with gifts, and I smelled gumbo.

My grandparents, my siblings and their spouses, and a few other family members were scattered around the room. I didn't expect this type of homecoming. I did everything they were against, and they celebrated me for it.

Mom took Ava as soon as we got all the way inside. She gave me a long hug. It blew my mind. I guess she got over the initial shock, but her wearing an ear-to-ear smile was not something I was used to. Mom showed off her granddaughter to everyone.

One of my mom's sisters and my grandparents greeted me with hugs and kisses. It was overwhelming. They all congratulated me on being a new mom. All of this shocked Aunt Vivica as well. We discussed it while eating two bowls of gumbo and saltines.

Mom hadn't put Ava down once. No one else could hold her. It was a beautiful thing to see. She was glowing. I took numerous pictures of them.

We played games, and they presented me with gifts for Ava. I didn't remember the last time I had such a good time. In the past, Trent came to my family functions, and it put a damper on my mom's mood. Whenever she didn't enjoy herself, no one could.

My sister said she had the biggest surprise for me after taking a phone call. She answered the door and then walked into the living room with Denise and Brian.

# CHAPTER SIX

"Aww, shit," Aunt Vivica not-so-quietly whispered with widened eyes.

It got my dad's attention. "Viv, watch your mouth. I am so sorry Momma Jones."

Aunt Vivica subtly pointed toward the foyer, and my dad turned around. My parents' house had a small foyer with a mirrored wall. The first opening was to the den and dining room. The second opening led to the living room where we all gathered together. Denise and Brian stood right at the living room entrance.

"Oh, shit!" dad exclaimed, but not as low as my aunt did. Mom chided him for his language. "I'm sorry, Honey. I thought a cockroach flew in behind B-Brian. They always try to get in the house."

Daddy and Aunt Vivica looked at me like they had seen a ghost. I felt the same damn way if not worse. My legs turned into jelly; I fell back onto the nearby wall.

Denise's smile turned into confusion. I watched her survey the room with extra attention on those two who caused a scene. Goodness!

"Hey," I said as if the last minute didn't happen.

Denise tilted her head. "Hey, yourself."

My legs somewhat cooperated as I made my way over to them. I nodded at Brian and side-hugged Denise because she held Layla.

"What are you guys doing here?" I asked.

"We ran into each other at the gym yesterday, so I told her to come over," my sister answered.

"Cool. So, um...yeah. I am visiting for a few days with my aunt."

"Kim, I thought you would be here for a couple weeks," my grandmother said.

I didn't realize how quiet the room had gotten. I thought music played in the background earlier, but I heard nothing. Someone needed to put something on the radio to drown us out a little. It was hard to lie with everyone listening.

"Yes, ma'am. I am."

"Kim, is everything okay? You don't seem thrilled that we're here," Denise said.

"Oh, no. It's not that. I'm just surprised and a little tired. It's been a long day."

We stood in the foyer with all eyes on us. "Look at your baby! She is adorable," I gushed.

"Thanks," Denise and Brian said in unison.

"Um...Are you guys hungry? My mom made gumbo," I informed them through my cracking voice.

"Sure, but who's Ava?" Denise asked, pointing to the banner behind me.

"Huh?" I let out.

"What? You don't know who Ava is? Kimberly, how is that even possible?" Mom asked.

Why the hell was everyone in our mouths? Mom walked over to us with Ava lying on her shoulder.

"This most beautiful little girl here is Ava. My first granddaughter. It's about time, right? I needed another little girl to spoil. Didn't I, grandma's baby?" she started talking to Ava.

Denise squinted her eyes and then stared at me with her mouth slightly ajar. "Wait, wait. Is she...she's *your* baby?"

"Huh?" I said again.

"Kim!" she pressed.

"Uh...yeah. She's mine."

Denise's eyes welled up. "Why didn't you tell me you were pregnant?"

We still stood where everyone heard every word. I put my hand on Denise's. I wanted to take her outside to talk. She yanked her hand away. "Why would you not tell me you had a baby?"

My mouth opened, but nothing came out. Brian placed his hand on his wife's shoulder.

"I am sorry, Denise. Can we talk about this in private?" I asked.

"No need. I see how it is." She tugged at Brian and walked toward the door.

"Stop! You don't understand, I—"

Denise turned back around. "You needed space, right? You got it." They walked out the door.

My family didn't even try to act like they minded their business. When I faced them, they stared at me, silent. I strolled into the kitchen to get a bottle of water and remove myself from their view.

After a few minutes, the attention veered toward the newest addition to our family. Ava saved me from anyone inquiring about what they witnessed.

🥀🥀🥀

BRIAN CALLED FOUR TIMES YESTERDAY. I assumed he had suspicions from the way he looked at me when he learned of my daughter. We had nothing to discuss. I didn't mean to hurt Denise, but I'd prefer her to be upset with me for not telling her about Ava than her finding out how Ava got here. I only had to avoid them until I got back to California.

Mom took me to lunch, and Ava stayed behind with Daddy. We had spent little time alone since I arrived a few days ago. Keisha met us at the restaurant which caught me by surprise.

The hostess led us to a small table at Mom's favorite restaurant, Pappadeaux. I suggested Razzoo's since it was only a few minutes down the road, but she insisted on Pappadeaux.

We placed our drink order, and I skipped the alcohol. Mom life blocked my fun already. I didn't pump a lot of milk and didn't want to take any chances. Plus, my mind should be clear for whatever these two schemed.

"So, how is California treating you?" Keisha asked.

Her actual question was, "what California man knocked you up?" She knew Trent wasn't the father after she questioned me about it before. Mom convinced herself of Ava being Trent's daughter. Maybe she couldn't force herself to believe I screwed another guy so soon after breaking up with him.

"It's nice! Peaceful. No one in your business kind of peaceful," I answered with a hard stare.

"Oh, okay. That sounds good and all, but don't you miss being home?" Keisha countered.

"Yes. However, I need the distance right now. Especially with Ava. I don't want to get caught up in any drama or anything. That is all I remember about home, the drama."

"Hmm, so there will be drama if you move back. I see," she said, peering from her side of the table.

"Ugh, I can't take all this. Who is Ava's father, Kim?" Mom demanded to know.

Finally. I wondered when someone would get to the point.

"Her dad is a guy I am not seeing. It was a one- time thing," I admitted.

"So, she really isn't Trenton's baby? Oh, thank God," Mom said, exhaling slowly.

"Mom, I told you that," Keisha said.

They had been talking about me?

"Yeah, but I thought you lied for your sister. So, who is he? Has he been around for Ava?" Mom probed.

"No. I lost contact with him. It's better this way."

"Is it really?" Mom looked at me as if she could see into my soul.

Not today. I guarded myself but also had to seem transparent so that my answers to these questions would only need to be said once. If my mom suspected anything, she'd keep asking until the answer changed. After a while, she'd believe it if the answer didn't waiver.

"Mom, please don't do that. You said it yourself that you needed a granddaughter," I reminded her.

"Not like this, I didn't. Don't get me wrong, I love my grandbaby. But how could you let this happen? Haven't you learned anything from your last relationship?" she asked.

Keisha pursed her lips. I bet she wished she was at another table right about now. I sure did. The waiter returned with our drinks and took our order. I got an appetizer that would probably go untouched.

"Mom, don't be too hard on her. I am sure this whole thing was stressful enough," Keisha told her, grabbing my hand under the table.

My baby sister had my back almost as much as my dad. She was always like that even as kids. I could handle myself, but she'd show me I wasn't alone.

"Can we talk about something else? I didn't come here for you to lecture me about having my baby who is already here. There is no use. I can't go back in time. I don't want to fall out with you again. You caused enough pain when I had my miscarriage."

"Hmph. I can't imagine what's worse. Having a baby with that boy or the possibility that you don't know her dad's last name."

"What did you say?" I asked, hoping she'd back down.

"You're in here talking about he's not in your life. Do you even know who he is? You moved to California to whore around? Now you are unmarried with a baby who will grow up with no father. I taught you better than this, Kimberly."

"Wait, what just happened?" Keisha asked with her hands up.

"Your mother happened. Man, I thought you'd be different this time," I said, standing up. I grabbed my purse.

"Where do you think you're going?" Mom asked.

"In case you haven't noticed, I am a grown woman. I don't have to take this kind of negativity

from no one. Not even my mother. I don't understand how you can be so...evil," I let out.

There wasn't any other word to describe her behavior toward me. Her hand flew to her chest. She was about to say something else.

"Please don't. Mom, I have tried my best to satisfy your impossible standards. I'm not doing it anymore. My mistakes are my own, not yours. You don't have to accept them. I still love myself. Ava is a blessing no matter how she got here. All I wanted is for you to see her that way, but you can't help yourself, can you?

"I'm so done apologizing to you for being human. Any consequences I have to face for my actions are mine and mine alone. Since the shame is too much for you to bear, I will keep them and us far away from you."

"Kim, wait," Keisha called out as I walked away from the table.

That woman would never change. She almost had me fooled, and I was a fool to think she'd be different. My baby was special, but even she couldn't perform the supernatural miracle my mom needed to be even a little happy for me.

I pushed the entrance doors open and walked through the courtyard. Keisha caught up with me by the water fountain.

"Nope! I am not going back in there with that woman so don't ask."

Keisha pointed to her purse. "I wasn't going to."

"What are you doing?"

"I cannot believe you called Mom evil." She burst out laughing. "You stood up to the queen. How does it feel?"

"Girl, what is wrong with you?"

"Nothing. I'm surprised, shocked, and...proud."

"What?"

"Kim, you are the only one who has the guts to talk back. You know Kendrick doesn't defend Tina when Mom goes in on her. Then I say nothing when she tries to tell us how to raise our son. But you ..." Keisha bowed.

"Stop it!" I saw people look at her.

"You called her evil!" She laughed again.

"Hell, it's the truth. Everything I do is so horribly wrong. Your mother can't ever see past her own close-minded self. Oh, and did you know she and Daddy got married when she was pregnant with me?"

"What?" Keisha's smile disappeared.

"Yeah. Aunt Vivica told me. Ooh, and I was waiting for her to call Ava a bastard child. I was going to get her with that one."

"Oh, my gosh! You are my hero," she told me, hooking my arm with hers.

"Whatever. I'm tired of Mom playing like she had this perfect life and that her children had to be the same. It's all bullshit."

"This is insane, girl."

"I know, but you'd better get back in there before she puts you on the naughty list too. You don't want to be on her bad side. She can get unreasonably ugly."

"When is she ever reasonable?"

"True. Still, don't get in trouble because of me."

"In trouble? In case you hadn't noticed, I'm a grown ass woman."

I laughed out loud. "I did not say it like that, crazy."

"Shoot, you might as well have. Did you see her face?"

"It's nothing new."

"Well, I am hanging with my big sister. Besides, your dramatic exit must have made you forget that you rode here with Mom."

We laughed.

"Why the hell you think I'm still standing here talking to you? I can't go nowhere."

"Ha! You stupid."

Keisha texted Mom that she was leaving with me. I joked that she was too scared to tell her to her face.

After we got into her car, I called Daddy to make sure everything was good with Ava. Since he'd recently put her down for a nap, I knew I had more time before I had to be back. So, we went to Razzoo's to eat since we walked out without food.

That evening, Daddy called himself having a talk with Mom. He got on me about being disrespectful and walking out on her. As bad as it was, it never crossed my mind that we stuck her with the bill. It took everything in me not to laugh in his face when he brought it to my attention. After everything she had said, that stupid check bothered her enough to tell Daddy.

I wanted to leave their house, and nothing would stop me. Our things were still in a suitcase. I asked my aunt to search for a nearby hotel. We were not staying here another night.

Aunt Vivica sat with me while I breastfed Ava to talk about what happened. At first, seeing my mom with my daughter blocked out all the reservations I had about coming back. It seemed like things were good. In Diana fashion, my mother proved me right and disappointed her sister-in-law.

My aunt booked a hotel room for us to share near First Colony Mall. It was the closest one that met her standards. Daddy tried to stop us and Mom ignored me as usual whenever she got in this kind of mood. He didn't want us to leave Houston sooner than planned. I assured him we'd stay as long as we originally intended, but I couldn't sleep in that house. Sometimes I wondered how he dealt with her.

Once we got packed up, Daddy drove us to the hotel. He helped us take our things up and the two of them left. Since we'd need a car, Daddy took his sister to rent one for the remainder of our visit.

I received a text from Denise to meet up somewhere today to talk. Aunt Vivica scheduled herself a spa day at the hotel, so I agreed to let Denise come over during that time. When she arrived, she wasn't alone.

Why the hell did she have to bring Brian?

Ava laid on a blanket on the floor, so Denise put Layla down with her. Layla was already moving around, grabbing at Ava's toys. It amazed me how three months made a huge difference in babies. They developed so fast in the first year.

Brian sat on the floor with the girls while Denise and I sat on the sofa. He glanced at me a few times after looking at the kids. Brian was a smart guy, but I was hoping that he'd be slow to notice anything.

"So, what is going on Kim? Why are we doing this?"

"Doing what?"

She rolled her eyes. "Don't play dumb. I didn't realize things were this bad. My baby shower came with no word from you. Then Layla was born, and you still didn't come to see me. Not even a call. You emailed me some funky congratulations crap, and that was it," Denise reminded me.

"Okay, I can see how—"

"The worst part of not having my best friend be there when I gave birth to my first child was how you didn't give me a chance to be there for yours. As hurt as I was, I would've shown up for you. Damn, Kim. I told you about my pregnancy before I told my momma."

"Dee, it's not that I—"

"No, don't! You had a baby. Can you understand how messed up that is? You were like my sister. First, you tell me you don't want to talk to me because of all the Trent drama, then you up and leave. None of it makes sense. Yes, you thought we were meddling in your relationship, but you seriously want to throw away almost all these years of friendship over it?"

"I'm sorry," I told her through trembling lips. Denise rolled her eyes and stared past me. "I've done some fucked up stuff to you. I am so, so sorry. I can't take it back or ever fix it. I figured it would be best if we moved on without each other. You don't need a person like me in your life, trust me. If you understood how deep all of this truly is, you'd hate me."

"Kim, there is nothing you could do to make me hate you," she naively suggested before placing her hand on mine.

I felt dirty. Brian looked pitiful over there listening to us. The truth would have to go to the grave as planned. Perfect, sweet Denise was oblivious to the terrible thing I had done with her husband. My stomach was in knots as she comforted me.

Everyone was on my back about going to hell for planning to live with Trent over a year ago. Well, hell may still be my destination for this shit.

Denise gave me a hug and my chest immediately burned. When she had let go, her eyes widened. "How did Trent take the news about being a dad? We haven't talked to him since you left either. Both of you guys wrote us off."

I cleared my throat then glanced at the kids. It hit me that Ava was spending time with her actual father.

"He's not her dad," I admitted.

"I'm sorry, what?" Brian said from the floor.

"Babe, can you let us talk?" Denise waved him off. "Kim, what is going on with you? You guys broke up a year ago. How is he not her dad?"

"There was a crappy night before I moved. Things went left, and I slept with some random dude. I was drunk and can't even remember the guy."

She covered her opened mouth with her hand. "Oh my."

"Yeah. Um...I didn't learn I was pregnant until later, but that's why I don't talk about him. So, it will only be the two of us. Plus, my aunt has been a tremendous help. We are good without him."

"Damn, girl. I never thought you'd be in this situation."

"It's fine. I made my bed. Everything else is on me. I'm happy I got my baby girl now."

Denise smiled while suggesting we play with the girls. I gagged on the inside as she held Ava. The tension between Brian and I grew once Denise mentioned how much the girls favored each other. Once she said they'd pass as sisters, Brian's face tightened.

Are they?" he asked.

Denise laughed. "How is that possible, silly boy?" She glanced my way, making circles around her ears mocking Brian. His eyes burned through me as we watched the girls. It didn't matter, he'd never find out.

Twenty minutes later, Aunt Vivica walked in. She almost hit the floor. I swear she and my dad were the worst when they needed to play it cool.

"Hello, hello," she said, letting the door close behind her.

Denise walked over to her. She introduced herself and her husband.

"Oh, yes. I remember you from some years back and, of course, a few days ago. I see you're visiting with Kim today. Caught up with everything?" Aunt Vivica asked, raising her brow at me.

"Yes. We didn't have time to talk the other night."

"Hmm. Is everything good, now?" she asked.

"I hope so. This niece of yours can be hard to understand sometimes."

"You don't know the half of it, honey," Aunt Vivica told her.

Brian waved before picking Layla up. I grabbed Ava and sat on a bed.

"Well, we'd better get going. I'm sure we will see you again before you leave, right Kim?" Denise asked.

"Uh, sure. Yeah, we can do that."

Denise narrowed her eyes. "See, I can't tell if she forgives me or not."

"Forgives *you*?" Aunt Vivica asked.

I hopped up. "The Trent stuff, Auntie. That's all."

She frowned while putting her things down on the table. "Is that right?"

There was no way they didn't pick up on her weirdness. Their faces said so.

"Mmhm. So, um…we will see you later. Y'all be careful," I told them, while handing Ava to my aunt.

I hugged Denise and tickled Layla before they left. Aunt Vivica put her free hand on her hip, tapping her foot when I turned away from the door.

"Don't look at me like that," I said flopping onto the empty bed. "Am I really such a horrible person?" I asked, but she said nothing. When our eyes met, she shrugged. Rolling my eyes and sighing, I whispered, "I am, huh?"

"Kim, this is bad. I mean bad, bad. Now, they are visiting you in the room? I'm not built to handle this kind of stuff. In

California, far away from it, I felt one way. Being in the same room with them and knowing what it truly is, I...I just don't know."

I groaned while flipping over onto my stomach.

"You gotta do something, say something. How will you be friends with her after what you and that man did? There's no way it sits well with you. It's messing with me, and I had nothing to do with it."

It didn't feel right, but I couldn't change it.

$$\wp\wp\wp$$

Our first week ended. Thank God! I was ready to leave. Mom still didn't speak to me but would take Ava from my arms whenever I walked into their house. At least my daughter didn't have to pay for my sins, according to the Almighty Judge Diana Duncan.

We pretended like nothing happened around my grandmother. She acted a lot like my mother, but she didn't ask questions about Ava's father. Maybe she assumed it was Trent like everyone else did. As long as those assumptions stayed in their heads and never reached Trent's ears, we were okay.

Tonight was a planned family game night. My sister and brother came over with their families.

Keisha got a once-over from Mom to make sure she understood, everything was a front.

Keisha told me she tried to talk to Mom hours after we left her at the restaurant but hadn't gotten a hold of her since. My little sister was too afraid to come to the house.

With my full experience of being on Mom's bad side, I told her she had nothing to fear. No one can disappoint my mother like me. As long as I was around, everyone else had the minimal effects of her wrath.

Mom busied herself with her grandchildren in the den

while the rest of us enjoyed a night of laughter. I forgot how mean my grandmother was when she lost a game. Daddy brought out *Guesstures*. We used to play this game every Thanksgiving.

Grandma would lose every single time. She was the worst at most games. Grandma gave her all trying to act out the words, but it made no sense. Whoever was on her team already accepted defeat before we started.

After that, we played *Pictionary* and *Jenga* before we separated into groups. Some gathered at the breakfast table for spades. Tina, Keisha, and I stayed in the living room.

We played pitty pat, speed, and double speed. After one round of double speed, they quit. My hands were too quick for them. We even played the 'I Declare War' card game. It was a much-needed night of fun. My mind deserved a break from the mess I had created.

Keisha suggested that we go to the rodeo that started this week. Tina got excited and said we should leave the kids with my parents. It would be a girls' outing. We hadn't done one of those in so long. I invited Aunt Viv to go with us. She said the rodeo used to be her favorite thing to do each year in her younger days.

ᗷᗷᗷ

THE NEXT MORNING, the ladies met us at my parents'. They beat us there, but were still outside. So, we all went into the house together with our kids. Daddy was the only one who knew about our plan, but my mom didn't mind. She loved her grandchildren.

I pumped enough milk for a whole day and placed it in the freezer. I kissed Ava goodbye and we headed out. To avoid parking fees for all of us, Keisha drove. This girl bought a three-row SUV, but claimed she didn't want anymore kids.

She only had one son. Her excuse when she got the truck was that she deserved it. My nephew turned two and terrible became his middle name. The car was her gift to herself for having to deal with him.

Tina sat in the front seat, Aunt Viv chose the second row, so I got stuck in the back since the car seat was also on the second row. Any time I said something, I had to yell over the air conditioner and the radio playing low in the background.

My text notifications dinged. Brian texted that he wanted to talk, but I ignored it. Then he claimed it was urgent in his last text.

"What is it?" I whispered. I didn't want my sister or Tina to hear my conversation.

"Why you sound mad?" he asked.

"I'm busy. I don't want to talk."

"Is it because of...you know?"

"If the 'you know' is the agreement we made that we would not communicate ever, then yes!"

"Okay. Listen, Denise is out right now, and I really need to talk to you. Can we meet somewhere?"

"Hell, no. Are you crazy?"

"Kim, it's not like that. I would never do that again."

"It should've never happened. I don't have time right now."

"Listen, this shit is killing me. I have to tell Denise."

"Don't do that! You guys will never have to see me again. When I am gone, it will be different. It's only a problem because we had to see each other in person."

"Denise makes it hard. She's always talking about you. All I can think about is that night whenever she brings you up."

"Is that why you called me?"

"No. Well, maybe. I want to ask you something, and I need you to be honest with me."

"Nope! I can't promise you that. I know what you're getting at so please don't."

"So, it's true."

"Nothing is true. At least not what you're thinking."

"Trent isn't your daughter's father."

"Stop right there. Stop! No one is, okay. She doesn't have one."

"Kim, am I—"

"I gotta go, bye."

I hung up. Why did we come here? We should've had my mom ride a bus or train and flew everyone else to California. Shit!

Aunt Vivica turned around in her seat. "That was him?"

"Yes."

"He knows?"

"No. He probably thinks it, but no."

97.9 The Box played on the radio. I squeezed my eyes shut. It's not like I could wish all of this away, but dammit I tried. At least the whole Brian part. He was a good guy with inexcusable judgment for one night. He was onto me.

When we arrived, I put my troubles on pause. The Houston Rodeo never got old. We didn't go to the concert because none of us cared for the band for the night. Honestly, the carnival was the best part, second to the food.

All of the heavenly aromas, from fried goodness to smoked everything, were in the atmosphere. Before we could explore with our taste buds, my aunt was drawn to the bungee jump setup near the entrance.

Tina and Keisha gave her the "hell no" look. She grabbed my hand and pulled me toward the empty line.

"Whoa! Uh-unh. I ain't doing that," I told her.

"Girl, stop being a wuss."

"I love you, but I am not jumping. It will snap and I will splatter all over the place."

"Kim, you have to get out of your head and be free every once and a while."

"Okay, that is great advice and all, but why do I always have to be free doing something that can kill me? You did that to me when we went zip lining. I think that is enough adventure for me."

"Punk."

"What? You do it then."

"I'm already free. You're the one who needs this experience."

"Ugh, fine. We can do it together," I said.

"No can do. I have grandkids that need me."

We laughed. How dare she try to talk me into it if she wouldn't do it too. I passed and we moved on.

There weren't a ton of people out since it was early, so we played a lot of games against each other. At least one of us won prizes every game. We rode most of the rides until it start filling up and the lines got too long.

That meant it was time to eat. I'd be taking on an extra ten pounds by the time we'd leave. I ate my absolute favorite food at the rodeo: boudain balls. They never failed to be the most delicious deep fried dish I've ever eaten.

The lemon pepper spiraled potato on a stick and fried snickers were also my go- to snacks. Aunt Vivica didn't believe me when I bragged about my favorites until she tasted them. She became a new fan of all three.

After almost four hours, we had done all we could do, spent a lot of money on things we didn't need, and ate more than we should have. My sister went hard on the frozen margaritas and beer. Even after all the food we ate, I didn't feel comfortable with her behind the wheel. I drove us home instead.

Daddy told me about his day with Ava and the boys while I got her things ready. I shared with him that Keisha should spend the night. The girl fell asleep in the back seat as soon as we left the parking lot. I called my brother-in-law and told him not to expect her tonight. He was glad she had a good time.

Tina left about thirty minutes after we got to my parents'. We left soon after. It wasn't even nighttime, but all the walking and greasy foods told my body it was time to lay it down. Daddy wanted us to stay longer. I couldn't do it.

We got back to the hotel with a sleeping baby and tiredness written all over our bodies. In the lobby, Brian and Layla were sitting in a chair. It stopped me in my tracks. Denise wasn't with them. Aunt Vivica asked one of the hotel employees for help with our things so she could get Ava. Then she nudged me to talk to him.

She walked away with a young man carrying our bags and left me standing there. Brian stood up and waited until I dragged myself over to him.

"What the hell are you doing here?"

"Kim, I know Ava's my baby."

"No the hell you don't. She is not yours. Like I told your wife, her father is not in the picture. I don't remember him."

"That's bullshit!" he whispered, covering Layla's ears as she rested her head on his shoulder.

"Watch it. You are wasting your time. Go home, Brian. Put your only daughter in the bed."

"Why are you lying?"

"How do you...Why do you think I would lie about that?"

"Because you love your secrets, Kim."

"Don't get smart."

"Whatever. You're not getting away with this lie. There's one fact you forgot about that you can't lie about."

"Like what?"

"Me! There's no way you slept with someone else before you left. You aren't even like that."

"I slept with you. That's proof enough that I can do dumb

stuff. Now, like I said, you are not my child's father. You need to go."

"She looks just like Layla and me."

"So, what? All babies look the same when they are born."

"No, they don't, Kim. Not this much."

"Whatever."

"Are you going to tell me the truth or not?"

"I already did. Ava's dad is dead to me."

"No, her dad is standing right in front of you."

"I'm not about to keep doing this with you, Brian. You are not her father. Why are you even doing this? You should be relieved she isn't yours."

"Sure, if that were true. I'm not crazy. You had to have gotten pregnant right after we..."

"I was with Trent too."

"No you weren't. He told me about it back then."

"I don't give a shit what he told you. I'm telling you now that we are not doing this. You are not her father. Now, go be a daddy to the one child you have and leave me alone."

I turned and walked away. Brian called my name a few times, but I kept going. I was doing both of us a favor by sparing the innocent. Why would he try so hard to prove something that would blow his entire world apart?

## CHAPTER EIGHT

# Brian

DENISE'S CAR SAT IN THE DRIVEWAY WHEN I PASSED by our house. I drove to Whataburger and got some food so she'd see why I wasn't home.

I kissed my wife after putting Layla in her crib. She removed our food from the bags.

"The line must've been long. I got here almost thirty minutes ago," she mentioned.

"Oh, uh, I couldn't make up my mind on what to get, so I drove around until I decided on a burger. I see you lost the garage door remote again."

"It fell between the seat and the console again. You have to get it for me. I couldn't."

"I got you. I'll get it before bed and put your car in the garage."

Denise kissed me. "Thank you, babe. For the chicken strips too. You should've gotten me a shake."

"It's right behind you."

She smiled. "You are the absolute best husband a woman could ever ask for."

"Not really."

"Ha! Yeah right. You know you are," she said, giving me another kiss before going to the kitchen table.

Denise grabbed the remote and put on one of those reality TV shows she loved watching. She'd always say it wasn't real because no one had that much drama in their life. As much as she felt they scripted it, she was hooked.

I feared our lives were about to get just as messy as the ones she watched play out on the screen. No matter how many times Kim denied it, something in me knew she was lying. We didn't use protection that night. Out of all the dumb things I had done, that night took the crown.

My wife was beautiful, sexy, thoughtful, loving, kind, and every other sought-after trait men wanted in a woman. I didn't deserve her from the moment we met because my heart was with someone else. After years of being with her, I fell in love with Denise. She was my everything.

Our relationship grew into something so beautiful once she became my best friend. I betrayed her in the worst way. My feelings for Kim were always there, but I had them under control and at one point I thought I had gotten rid of them.

That fucking night had me all screwed up, but I let it happen. Kim tried to stop me more than once, and she was the inebriated one.

It had been years since I thought about Kim the way I did when we first met. My shot disappeared as soon as Trent came into the picture. I had her all to myself before that and should've gone for it. We wouldn't be here if I did. If there were no regrets, none of this would've ever happened. Even so, I should have never acted on it. My wife was my world.

The next day, I sent Denise off to a spa day at Hotel ZaZa. She wasn't the type to pamper herself, so I made sure she'd have the whole day being waited on. My wife did so much for me, Layla, and her family.

My in-laws moved back to Atlanta with her grandmother

who pulled through last year. No one saw that coming. They were all prepared to bury her, but she recovered. Denise's mom did not want to be so far away, so they packed up and moved.

My wife took it hard, and I knew deep down she wanted to leave too. Because she had such a giving heart, she couldn't ask me to move since my whole family lived in or near Houston. I would've gone, but she wouldn't allow it. Instead, she flies there every two or three weekends. We've gone twice as a family.

Today would be all about her winding down and relaxing. It would also be about me finding answers. I reached out to Trent to meet up. If Kim wouldn't be straight with me, Trent would.

We found a parking spot at Kitty Hollow Park near the playground. Since I had Layla all day, it had to be somewhere she'd enjoy. Being only six and a half months old, she liked the baby-sized swing.

Trent walked over to us close to ten minutes later. "What's up man," he said harshly. We hadn't spoken since we somewhat fought.

"Everything, but I didn't come here to talk about that. I need to ask you something," I told him while pushing Layla in the swing.

"What is it?"

I glanced at him for a moment. He looked pissed and seemed like he wanted to be somewhere else. It was messed up how we fell out. We grew up together, and I missed my brother.

"Kim is back in town."

"Man, please tell me you didn't call me out here to—"

"With a baby."

For a minute, Trent went silent. Then he exhaled loudly.

"A baby?" He clasped his hands behind his head as he turned away. "What the fuck?" he mumbled.

"Denise and I saw her twice and she claims the father isn't in her little girl's life. She wouldn't say anything else about it. I assumed the baby was yours. She had her not long after our daughter was born."

"So, you telling me I have a baby with Kim?"

"I'm saying, she is back and has a kid. She won't say who's the father. I wanted to tell you in case you are."

"I bet you did. Same old Brian. Always in Kim's business. This time, it has nothing to do with me."

"Why you say that?"

"Man, we always used condoms. She wouldn't let me get near her without one. It can't be me."

"Really?"

"Kim mentioned another dude before she left. I thought she was joking. Maybe the kid's his. We ain't do much before we ended things."

"Oh. Damn. My bad, man. I guess I called you out here for nothing."

"Guess so." Trent placed his hands in his pockets. His keys jingled which I assumed meant he was ready to go.

"Look, before you leave, I want to apologize for hitting you like that. It was a crazy time, and I was tripping."

"I was trippin' harder. I said some fucked up shit, and I kind of deserved it. That shit won't happen again though. Gotta watch you quiet muthafuckas. Y'all be catching people off guard."

We laughed. I was glad to have at least said that much to Trent. Not seeing my brother in over a year was difficult. Our pride was to blame. Even six months ago, I wouldn't have admitted to having anything to apologize for. Denise drilled it in my head that I went too far when I hit him.

Once his guard came down, he got a closer look at Layla.

He shared what's been going on with him, I did the same. Trent mentioned Kim a lot and how he thought about trying to get her back after he grew tired of all the women he'd been with. The lifestyle he desired wasn't as glorious as it appeared.

In the back of my mind, I saw and felt Kim. She was his woman for so many years. It didn't matter if I had her first for that one night or if I loved her more than he ever could. We crossed a forbidden line.

When everything comes out, there will be casualties. Telling my wife was one thing, but it never dawned on me that I stabbed my brother in the back. They weren't together at the time, but that wasn't the point. Kim might be right, I shouldn't tell Denise. I still hadn't found out if Kim's little girl was actually my daughter.

After twenty minutes, Layla became fussy, and we left the park. Trent and I agreed to keep in touch. If what I thought was true, then that wouldn't be the case soon.

Late that afternoon, I found myself at Kim's parents' doorstep. Layla was with Denise. I told my wife I was going to the gym to play basketball. So, there I stood, dressed to hoop as I hesitated. What was I going to say?

Convincing myself this was a bad idea, I walked back to my car. Halfway down the driveway, Mr.

Duncan pulled up in his truck. Since he caught me in his yard, it would be rude to get in my car and leave without speaking. When he exited his vehicle, he looked at me solemnly.

"Hi, Mr. Duncan."

"How are you doing, son?"

"I'm good, sir."

"Good, good." He nodded and leaned against his truck. "So, you must've talked with Kim."

"Yes, sir. I talked to her yesterday."

"Mmm. How are you and your wife taking it? I can understand it's a lot to process."

"What do you mean, sir?"

His eyes widened. He took off his sunglasses and pinched the bridge of his nose. "She didn't tell you?"

"Tell me what?" I wanted to hear him say the words.

Mr. Duncan cleared his throat. "Why are you here? Are you looking for Kim?"

"Yes, but I think you answered the question she wouldn't."

"No, I didn't."

"Mr. Duncan, please. Ava is my daughter, isn't she?"

"Son, that is for you and my daughter to discuss."

"I tried to. Kim keeps telling me it's a random guy, but Ava looks like my daughter, Layla."

Mr. Duncan scratched his head and then pulled out his cell phone. From what I heard, Kim was on the other end, and he told her to come outside. Seconds later, she walked out the front door. I watched her stop and even take a step back when she saw me next to her dad.

"Nope. Get over here, young lady."

"Daddy, what are you doing?" she whined, walking toward him.

"Now, I don't understand why you have made a choice to lie to this man, but I won't. We talked about this many times. I expect you to do the right thing, Kimberly. Do it for that beautiful, joyful little girl in there. Make this right."

"Yes, Daddy," Kim said reluctantly.

Her father grabbed three plastic bags of groceries from his truck and went into the house. Kim stood in front of me with her hands in her shorts' back pockets, staring at the ground.

"What did he say to you?" she asked after almost a minute of silence.

"He said what you wouldn't. Now I know the truth."

"The truth about what?" she asked, looking to her left and avoiding eye contact.

"Kim, stop this. You know what I'm talking about. Ava is my daughter."

Her face tightened for a moment before tears fell down her cheeks. I stepped closer; she moved further away. "So, now what?" she asked, wiping her tears and shrugging.

"What do you mean?"

"Look, I don't want to hurt Denise any more than we already have. Whether or not she knows, I can't even sleep at night knowing what we did and the consequence. I love Ava with everything in me, but she's here because of our messed up actions. We can't say anything."

"Kim, I can't ignore the fact that you have my child. I won't."

"Please, don't make this harder than it has to be. We don't need anything from you, Brian. You can have a happy life with your wife and make more babies. We will have our happy lives in California and will never bother you for anything," she said, looking at me.

"You're serious?"

Kim answered with a nod and a straight face. How could she think I'd go along with any of this?

"I can't do that," I told her.

"Why not? If my dad didn't open his mouth, we wouldn't be here. Just pretend like this never happened," she said, walking away.

I jogged toward her and grabbed her hand to pull her back. When she faced me, I wrapped my arms around her, and she cried more onto my chest. I held her tighter.

"Don't do this, okay? You don't have to do this alone. I want to be there for my daughter."

She pushed me away. "You can't."

"What do you mean I can't?"

"Brian, we cannot tell Denise. My family doesn't know besides my dad and my aunt. I had no intentions on ever telling you. I don't want to mess up anything else."

"We both did this. It's not on you. I'm the one who fucked up. I can't act like none of this ever happened. It will haunt me more than cheating on my wife."

"Why do you have to be so fucking honest about everything? You can't lie one time?"

"Do you hear yourself? You're asking me to neglect my daughter to save face. I won't be able to live with myself knowing my child is growing up without her father. I'm not a coward. I will not ignore her like some deadbeat."

"You're not getting it. You have a child with your wife's best friend. Well, used-to-be best friend. The perfect woman will have her heart ripped out of her for what? Your marriage will be over. She will hate us forever for this."

As much as I fought to be right, she had a point. Denise didn't deserve any of this. She gave me all of her, and I gambled it away in one night. The love of my life and mother of my first-born child would pay the highest price for my transgressions.

Even though I never meant for any of it to go down like this, it still wasn't enough to break Ava's heart if she had to grow up thinking her dad didn't love her. I barely knew her, and I'd die for her right now because my blood was flowing through her little body. She was in this world partly because of me.

How could I walk away?

I WAS BEYOND READY TO GET OUT OF THIS DAMN city.

Sheryl called me yesterday and invited me to have lunch today. She found out I was in town and wanted to catch up.

When I met with her, she was disappointed because she expected to see Ava. It threw me off. I was positive that my daughter never came up in any of our conversations.

After talking a few minutes, she shared that Brian told Trent I had a kid. I was going to kill him. This kind of shit was why I wanted nothing to do with him or his wife before I moved away.

Sheryl convinced herself that she had a granddaughter now, and I had to burst her bubble. I gave her the same answer everyone else got about the father not being in our lives and that Trent was not her dad.

She didn't buy it. Sheryl wasn't rude about it since she was aware of everything that went down with her son and me. The only thing she requested after hearing my explanation was for Trent to take a paternity test.

"Sheryl, we don't need a test. I am one thousand percent sure your son is not Ava's dad. Trust me."

"I don't know, girl. You might not tell us if he was so you wouldn't have to deal with him."

"Now, I love you too much to lie about this. If you were my daughter's grandmother, I would've told you during my pregnancy. Our relationship means a great deal. Hell, life would be less complicated if she was for Trent."

"Well, when you say it like that, I don't have a choice but to accept it. And I love you too. So, who is this mystery man? Do I know him?"

"I hope not."

She laughed. Lying to her sucked, but the truth was more than ugly. She could lose respect for me if she found out. This mess affected every relationship I had. Even if most of my loved ones didn't hold it against me forever, their knowledge of my wrongdoing would make them see me differently.

We sat in the middle of the restaurant talking about the highs of our past year. Then Trent hugged me from the back of my chair and kissed my cheek before taking a seat.

Trent was the absolute last person I wanted to be around. The smirk on his face was reason enough to avoid this stupid meeting. He, of all people, knew we did not have a baby together. I allowed no slip-ups with him after my miscarriage. Yet he sat beside me asking about my daughter as if he wanted to catch up on everything he missed.

"Sheryl, I am sorry, but this is a waste of time. Trent is not my daughter's father. Everyone wants to believe it since me being with someone else seems far-fetched. The fact is, I was. Another man was in the picture on a drunken night, and now I have his baby, not your son's."

"Did you cheat on me or something?" Trent asked.

"Nope, that was all you playa. I did what I did after we broke up."

"Yeah right, I suspected you were fucking somebody else when you stopped sleeping with me," he claimed.

"Boy, watch your damn mouth. I'm right here," Sheryl said, popping him behind his head.

"He is who he is. Besides, we both know I wasn't sleeping with you because you were doing God knows what with your little side chick."

"You still salty about that, I see."

"No, I'm not. It's only the truth. You got a problem with the truth?" I said looking at him.

"Mmhm. Let's see if he can be honest about his current situation," Sheryl stated.

"Ma, don't do that," he told her.

"What are y'all talking about?" I asked.

Sheryl nudged him. "Mr. Player over here is burnt out from his hoes."

I burst out laughing.

"Momma!"

"It's okay, Trent. Kim's family. Even if you couldn't treat her right," she told him.

"You are something else. Your son got what he wanted," I said.

"Girl, he is too much. I wish you two could get back together. It would make him grow up."

"Uh-unh, I already got one kid to take care of. I'm not ready for two," I told them.

"Dang, you think I'm gonna knock you up that quick."

"No, fool. She's saying *you* are the other kid," Sheryl clarified.

"No offense to you. You are an amazing woman and mother."

"None taken. I only take responsibility for his good qualities. The rest is from his idiot father."

We all laughed. I enjoyed times like these. She treated me

like a person and not an embarrassment. If only my mother acted this cool. The best part was I didn't need her son to still have her. She was a true friend.

After the first ten minutes, I wanted this lunch to be over. Now I wished it didn't have to end. We talked about good times, but I reminded Trent of the bad ones. He apologized a lot, and I forgave him. I owned up to my part since he wasn't the only one wrong all the times we were at odds.

The food came, and we finished up an unexpected highlight of this trip. Spending time with Trent never amounted to anything but an argument. I appreciated the shift. We wouldn't be best friends or anything, but it was nice to catch up.

After lunch and showing Sheryl many requested images of Ava, we parted ways. She gave me a long embrace when I explained that I wouldn't visit Houston for a long time. Trent almost got slapped after stealing a kiss when we hugged.

Brian received a call with my voice yelling on the other end. I didn't want Sheryl or Trent to hear about any of this, but Brian had to go running his mouth again. This time he had no excuse. He did that shit on purpose, claiming he only met with Trent to see if he could be Ava's father. Why did everyone care so damn much? She was *my* child.

Brian wanted to visit Ava and me for an hour. Denise had a hair appointment in the evening, so he figured it was enough time for him to secretly see my daughter.

When I told Aunt Vivica about it, she almost looked as judgmental as my mother. She offered to leave for the visit and hang with her brother so we'd have the hotel room to ourselves. My aunt joked that we'd better not make any more babies while she was away. I didn't find it funny, but she cracked herself up.

A little after six o'clock, Brian knocked on my hotel room door. He had Layla with him and walked right past me to get to Ava, who was laying in her portable bassinet. I put a blanket and some toys down for Layla after he sat her on the bed. I didn't need her falling off and hurting herself.

Brian wore the brightest smile I'd ever seen on him when he lifted Ava out of the bassinet. She would never remember this strangely adorable moment. Tears wanted to come out until reality kicked back in.

I sat on the bed closest to the door, watching Layla play on the blanket. She was such a beautiful little girl. I cringed when I noticed how much she looked like an older Ava. I hoped Ava would develop more features from my side. She was too young to determine who'd she would take after, so I still had time.

Ava smiled as Brian spoke to her. He told her he was sorry for not being around when she first came into the world and that he missed the first months of her life. He promised her he wouldn't miss anything else. I wasn't so sure about that, but I let him have it for the moment.

Brian's eyes filled with tears that didn't fall. The tissue box was close, so I grabbed it for him.

"She's so perfect," he said while pressing the tissue on his eyes.

"Yeah, she is. So is Layla. She got big quick, huh?"

"A little too quick. Not so long ago, we brought her home from the hospital, and now she's eating baby foods and trying to get around on her own."

"That's crazy."

He carefully sat on the floor next to Layla. She scooted her way over to him, so he picked her up. "Layla, this is your little sister, Ava."

It felt like someone squeezed my heart. "Um, can you not do that?"

"Do what?"

"The whole sister thing. I understand that it's true. It sounds so wrong. Hell, it is wrong."

He sucked his teeth. "It's not like they know what I'm saying, Kim."

"So. I do, and I don't like it."

"They will learn about each other one day. Stop tripping."

"I'm not tripping. You are. You up in here acting like everyone will be okay with all of this. We ain't about to be some big happy family. Get that through your head already."

"What is your deal? Do you need to be so negative all the time?"

"Since when did honesty become a negative thing?"

"You don't have to keep reminding me of the messed-up situation. I get it, damn!"

"Don't cuss at me."

"Then stop being so..."

Layla grabbed the bottom of his mouth and then his lips. She wanted him to shut up as much as I did. His little girl most likely saved him from getting cussed out and kicked out.

"Quit telling me how to act with my daughters, okay."

"Whatever. All that happiness will go down the drain if you run your mouth to Denise."

"There you go again. I want to spend time with *our* daughter without having to hear all of that."

It irked me to hear him say "our daughter." She was all mine only a week ago. I wished we had never come here.

We would've had a pleasant visit if Keisha hadn't run into Denise and told her about it. I didn't blame my sister. She was in the dark like everyone else. I should've presumed this trip wouldn't go on without a hitch.

Some kind of way I'd have to persuade Brian not to tell his wife about his newfound daughter. The one thing I admired about him was his honesty, and now it was the only thing that determined what type of relationship we'd have. All he had to do was keep this knowledge to himself. He'd get all the pictures and videos of Ava. I'd make sure he wouldn't miss anything.

He held both the girls in his arms and talked to them as if they understood a single word he said. The gist of the speech was about him always being there for them no matter what happened. I predicted part of what would occur if he broke the news to Denise about Ava.

"Can we be serious for a minute?" I asked.

He exhaled. "Sure."

"Are you really going to tell Denise?"

"Didn't we already go over this?"

"Not enough if you still plan on telling her."

"I admit it's hard to confront people when you make mistakes but there's no other choice. It's been hard since she still believes I'm the perfect husband. Every time she looks at me with so much love in her eyes, I imagine it all being taken away when I come clean. That's the only reason I haven't said anything yet."

"Then don't. I'm telling you it's for the best. Denise had already suffered through postpartum depression, right? What the hell do you think this will do to her? What will it do to your marriage?"

"The question is what will happen to my daughter if I listen to you and ignore the fact she exists? How would you feel when she finds out you were the reason her father wasn't around? Your inability to put anyone before yourself will ruin our child's life. I'd bet money she'd take years to forgive you."

"Okay, that is so over-the-top. She will have her mother and maybe even a stepdad someday. I don't plan on being single forever. Ava will be fine."

"A stepdad? She has a father, Kim. Why can't you let—"

"You don't get it!" I raised my voice. "Your wife is who I am more concerned with, Brian. I am more worried about her than you are."

"You don't know her like I do. She will forgive us, and over time, everything will be fine."

"Man, you are delusional."

"Excuse me?"

"You're crazy if you categorize this as a lightweight problem. This is not something someone will say 'oh, it's okay, I understand.'"

"Now I get why Trent said you were impossible to talk to. You only see things your way. Everybody doesn't think the way you do, Kim. You are not always right."

"Wow! It's time for you to go."

"So, you can talk all your nonsense for days, but I can't tell you the truth about yourself for one second before you kick me out."

"Put my daughter down and get out."

"She's my daughter too."

"I don't care."

He stood up with the bed's help and a baby in each arm. Then he sat across from me on the other bed. "It will not be the end of the world. Trust me. Denise will be rational about it, and I will do everything in my power to help her get to a place where she can one day forgive us for this. And she will do just that."

"For your sake, I hope you are right. My experience says otherwise, but you stay with that theory and call me when it comes true."

"It will. My wife is damn near perfect. There isn't a hateful bone in her body."

"A woman is usually near perfect when she's ignorant to the things her man does behind her back. Once she knows, she isn't the same. Trust me on that."

"Look, we are not you and Trent. We—"

"Say his name one more gotdamn time, Brian. Your ass

will be on the other side of the door," I told him, pointing to his soon-to-be exit.

He stopped talking.

"I want to protect Denise from further damage, but you are her husband. You do what you decide is best. Give me a heads up when you do it so I can take cover. I'd prefer it if you wait until I leave."

"You aren't going to live in California for good, are you?"

"Why wouldn't I?"

"How am I supposed to be in Ava's life? Can't you move back here?"

"Hell, no."

"Why not? That isn't fair for anyone. Why are you being so selfish? Ava's life matters more than your comfort. She needs her father."

"Let's be very clear about something. The truth about us had the grave as its destination. Unfortunately, you found out about it, but that doesn't change how I will live my life with my daughter. Moving back was never an option and still isn't."

"You can't do that. She's my daughter too."

"Watch me."

My aunt opened the door. I wanted him to get the hell out. She asked if we needed more time. I answered no, he said yes. Then he explained to her what I had told him.

At first, she told him she didn't want to get involved in our business. Aunt Vivica had my back, so either way, he'd be in the wrong. Brian needed to get with the program and accept we were not staying. He insisted my aunt tell us her opinion about it all. She ended up siding with Brian.

Aunt Vivica made it known months ago that she didn't agree with me keeping Ava's father a secret. She explained to him that if she were in my shoes, she would not move so far away with a new baby when her father wanted to be a part of her life. No one discussed how Denise would take it and it bothered me.

Brian and Auntie double-teamed me about Brian wanting to be a good dad. Neither of their input mattered. My life, my choice.

To keep the peace, I told them I'd consider what they said knowing damn well I wouldn't. All my daughter needed was at least one happy parent. Two would be ideal, but it was out of the question.

# *Brian*

I couldn't comprehend Kim's stubbornness. My daughters deserved to have their father around. The drive home was better since Kim at least had a sane person around her. Ms. Vivica would keep her grounded.

Soon enough, my wife had to know what we got ourselves into. If the possibility of all this occurred to me that night with Kim, I would not have gone through with it. Kim had a piece of my heart for so long, and I figured that one more time couldn't hurt anything. It was apparent we wouldn't tell anyone since we kept our first time to ourselves.

Denise made everything so easy and I complicated our lives for moments of pleasure. The guilt of my actions felt like a cloud following me around. My wife was living in sunshine and bliss unbeknown to her, I had broken our vows. If she's the woman I knew she was, she'd still keep hers, and we would work through this.

When I opened the garage door, Denise was getting out of her car. I couldn't drive off this time, she looked dead at me. Plus the garage opening was a giveaway of my arrival. I pulled in and got out to unbuckle Layla.

"Where are y'all coming from?" Denise asked.

"The park."

"This late?"

"Well, we were laying on the grass looking at the stars. She fell asleep on me while I was teaching her a little about astronomy," I answered, walking through the door to our laundry room.

"That stuff puts her to sleep too, huh?" she teased.

I complimented Denise's hairstyle and followed her to our bedroom with Layla asleep in my arms. After laying her in the crib, Denise and I entered our bathroom. She continued walking to the closet while I used the water closet. The events at the hair salon were all she talked about while changing.

I washed my hands as she finished dressing before we tiptoed back through our bedroom to go to the kitchen.

"Are you hungry?" she asked.

"I don't think so."

She raised an eyebrow. "What kind of answer is that?"

"Oh, I'm not that hungry right now."

"You want me to cook something anyway?"

"No, babe. That's okay. I'll make a sandwich later."

"Are you sure? I can make breakfast since it's quick."

"I'm okay, beautiful."

"Alright. Don't ask for any of my food then."

We laughed. I had a history of being more hungry than I thought when she'd only make enough for herself.

"I won't."

"Sure you won't. I'm making me a breakfast burrito and only one."

"I'll take one then. You can make it however you make yours."

"Mmhm. That's what I thought."

I sat on the couch and turned the TV on while she cooked. When I stopped on ESPN, she told me I'd have to turn it off when she finished. There were recorded shows she wanted to catch up on while she ate.

Denise glowed while preparing the food. She smiled the whole time and sang under her breath. I pondered over what Kim said. Would the truth turn my wife into a different person? Yeah, she'd be beyond furious and hurt, but it wouldn't be as bad as Kim claimed.

There were a few more days before Denise would learn about my illegitimate daughter. Ava should be back in California by then.

It's not like I worried about anyone's safety the way Kim did, but if they weren't here, then all the anger would be taken out only on me. I deserved it more than anyone else.

We ate dinner and split up. She watched her shows and I retreated to my office. Layla woke up for about two hours. Denise gave her a bath and fed her before she fell back asleep.

My wife kept asking if I was okay. So many times I wanted to tell her no, but then I'd have to explain why. Seeing her now and imagining how she'd be afterward scared me. Breaking my baby's heart was the last thing I ever wanted to do and being honest about this would make heartbreak inevitable.

We fell asleep watching a movie in bed. All of a sudden, Denise hugged me from behind. That was my cue to turn around and hold her, so I did.

My wife pressed her soft, warm lips against mine. When she slid her hand into my boxers, I knew what time it was. Foreplay wasn't her thing most of the time. I appreciated not having to do the extra work every time we made love. She wrapped her hand around the tip and stroked it. Once I moaned, she pulled the covers back and straddled me.

"Do you know how much I love you?" she whispered.

I said nothing because she was still rubbing up and down my shaft. She leaned forward and kissed me before gently biting my ear. Then she kissed my neck down to my chest. She scooted back further down my legs and put her mouth on the tip. I bit my lip and then Kim's touch popped up in my head.

"No, stop," I told her.

She snickered. "What? Are you worried about Layla? She won't hear us. We'll be quiet."

I sat up. "Baby, I can't."

"What are you talking about?" she asked.

"I can't do this."

She stopped moving and got off of me. The light from the TV illuminated her confused face. "What's the problem?"

"If I tell you, you will leave me."

She laughed and hit my shoulder. "You are so dramatic."

"Baby, I'm serious. I can't do this anymore. I have been lying to you about something and...I need you to promise you won't divorce me if I tell you."

She sat up straight and placed her hand on my shin. "Okay, now you are scaring me."

I adjusted my boxers. "I'm not trying to."

"Why are you acting weird? Did you get fired or something?"

"No. It's nothing like that."

"Oh. Well, what is it?"

"Promise me first."

"Ugh, I promise, boy. Now what is so horrible that's supposed to make me leave you?"

The TV's brightness bounced around the room. It made her eyes sparkle. My pulse sped up.

"Last year I kind of, um...See, I had...I slept with Kim," I confessed.

Denise laughed out loud. "Be serious. What is it?"

"That's what it is."

"Wait, tell me again. You did what?"

I took a deep breath and braced for a punch or slap or whatever else would be her natural reaction.

"I slept with Kim," I repeated in a rush.

"Brian, don't play games like that. It's not funny." Her face changed from laid back to serious.

"Babe, I am telling you the truth."

"I don't understand. What are you saying right now?" she asked, rubbing her forehead.

"Kim's daughter is mine."

The few seconds of silence felt like minutes.

"No, she's not. Why you would even say something like that?"

"Denise, on everything I love. I am not lying to you. I couldn't go another night with this weight on my chest. It's killing me to keep this from you."

She got out of the bed and left the room. I took a few deep breaths before I did the same. Denise stood in the middle of the living room with crossed arms over her chest. When I was a few feet away from her, she looked up at me.

"Brian Jerome Taylor, you'd better tell me what the hell is going on."

"Last year, I slept with Kim, and now we have a daughter."

"No, you didn't," she said, shrugging her shoulders hard.

"Yes, I did. I am so sorry, babe."

"No, you didn't. You would never ever do something like that. You wouldn't."

When I didn't respond, tears flowed down her cheeks. I stepped closer to her. After the third step, she slapped me.

"You didn't sleep with her. My best friend? Tell me you're lying."

I looked into her eyes so she'd understand it wasn't a lie.

"Brian, what the fuck?" She put her hands on her forehead and then on her stomach. "I'm gonna be sick."

My wife ran to the guest bathroom and slammed the door. I walked to the hall next to the bathroom and waited for her to come out. I heard the toilet flush, then the faucet turned on and off. Minutes later, she was still in there.

"Denise, are you—"

"No! Don't say anything."

"Babe."

"Do not talk to me right now."

I didn't. I sat on the floor and leaned back against the wall and waited. Denise was crying, but she wouldn't let me do anything to help her.

"Babe, I can't tell you how sorry I am. It should have never happened."

The bathroom door swung open, but she didn't come out. I got onto my feet and kept my distance.

"What can I do to—"

She put her hand up, gesturing me to stop. The way she looked at me was something I had never experienced with her. I hoped this wasn't Kim's prediction already coming true. Her expression gave me the impression she'd burst into flames at any second.

"Am I supposed to believe my husband fucked my best friend? And has a baby with her? Is that what you just said?"

I kept quiet. I didn't want to confirm it again.

"Brian," she yelled. Her booming voice made me jump. "Answer me."

I moved toward her. "Denise, I'm so sorry."

"Don't you dare come near me. Don't you ever touch me again. Matter of fact, don't talk at all. I am getting my baby and leaving."

"In the middle of the night?"

"I will not spend another minute in this house with you."

When she walked past me, I raced to block her from our bedroom door. From the way she glared at me, I braced for another blow.

"Get the fuck out of my way," she demanded.

"No, wait! I will leave for the night. I don't want you out there this late. I'll go."

"Don't act like you care if something happens to me. You don't love me."

"Yes, I do, Denise. More than anything."

She stepped back and placed her hands on her head. "With Kim? Of all the women in the world, you cheated with Kim?"

"Denise, please?"

"Both of you can burn in hell and on earth, I don't care. You are dead to me." She tried to get to our door again.

"No. I told you I will go. Don't wake Layla up. I will go."

"Oh, my God! Her daughter is your kid? Yours?"

I said nothing. The disgust in her voice and her eyes made my body ache.

"You knew all this time? And you had—"

"I didn't."

"Yeah right."

"She admitted it a couple days ago."

She cocked her head back and closed her eyes before squatting with her hands behind her neck. "You fucked Kim, and she just let you."

"It wasn't her fault. She tried to stop me."

"What the fuck are you saying? You forced her?"

"No! Not like that. I..."

"Forget it. Don't tell me. When are you leaving?"

"Right now. I'll go now."

"Hold up. Did you do it in our house?"

"No. Of course not."

"Of course not? You say it like that makes it any better that you screwed her somewhere else."

"Denise, can—"

"Leave," she screamed. Layla whined, but only for a few seconds. I walked to the door to check on her. Denise rushed over and pushed me away from it. "Get out, now."

"I need to change."

"No, you don't. You need to get the fuck out now."

"Babe, I need a shirt at least."

Denise crossed her arms over her chest and stood firm in front of our bedroom door. "You are so lucky we didn't get that gun."

The way she looked at me, I believed her. I pictured myself laid out bleeding to death if we had one. I got a jacket from the coat closet and put on my dirty lawn cutting shoes. Good thing I had on pajama pants. Otherwise, I'd have to sleep in my drawers in the car somewhere.

My car keys were on the counter next to my wallet. Denise mumbled something, but still stood her ground at the bedroom door.

"Can I get my phone from the room?"

She didn't answer me with words. It was clear I had to leave without it. I sat in the car for some minutes before driving away. I did it. My wife knew the sinful secret that felt like a ton of cement on my back. In no way did I feel better about any of it.

On the way to the nearest hotel, I stopped by a 24-hour Walmart and bought underwear, deodorant, a toothbrush travel kit, and something to throw on tomorrow. I checked in at the Quality Inn not too far from home.

When I got into the room, I fell back onto the bed and closed my eyes. Sleep was far from my mind. My heart was beating so hard, it's like I'd been running.

My wife's eyes blazing through me invaded my thoughts. If only this were a nightmare that would be over as soon as my eyes opened. What the hell was I thinking? Kim was right, and I hated to admit it this early on, but Denise spewed hatred from her entire being.

Things would have been better if she was the one who

cheated. I'd rather be cheated on than to be the cheater. It tore me apart.

My actions came at a price I wasn't mentally ready to pay. It was only the first hour, but something about the way she spoke made it evident that I underestimated this whole thing. My wife's heart crumbled right before my eyes, and it killed me. I couldn't unsee it.

My life flashed by in minutes. Past, present, and future. It played out one way, and I shook my head to think of a different scenario. None of them were realistic if they had a happy ending. The happiness drained from my house as soon Denise realized I did the unthinkable to our family. The pain in her eyes, the tears, her voice, all of it kept me awake until the morning.

I used the hotel phone to tell Denise I was coming home. She didn't answer. All I thought about was that she used last night to pack up and leave. The image of an empty home caused me to rush through traffic and speed past every yellow light. I didn't need a ticket wasting more time and giving her a better head start.

Her car was still parked inside the garage once it opened. I exhaled for what seemed like the first time since I left the hotel.

As I unlocked the door, I braced myself for whatever she wanted to throw at me literally and figuratively. I couldn't believe my eyes when I stepped inside. It looked like there had been a struggle. The place was a mess.

I imagined the worst-case scenario. I shouted her name and ran past the clothes and smashed electronics to get to our bedroom. Our room was untouched while she and Layla sat on the bed.

"Are you okay? What happened?" I asked, rushing to her side.

Layla reached for me, but Denise pulled her back. She

never looked my way. "I'm not okay. You happened. I do feel a little better but not enough for you to be in my face."

I backed away and left the room. Denise knocked my seventy-inch flat screen to the floor. I lifted it and saw the shattered screen. My PS4 and Xbox One looked like she smashed them with a hammer or something.

The clothes all over the floor were only mine. At least I didn't smell bleach. When I grabbed a pair of jeans, I saw the rips in them. The shirt next to it had the same damage. She had cut up all of my clothes.

There was nothing I could do about any of it. I couldn't be mad either, I deserved worse and was sure to get it sooner than later. The bedroom door opened, but it was Layla. Denise must have put her on the floor. I walked over and picked her up, holding her tight. I went to my nightstand to get my phone that was on the charger when I left last night. It was gone.

I didn't want to ask, but I had to. When I did, Denise pointed to the bathroom. The closet had a similar mess as the rest of the house. I passed the water closet but stepped back because I saw the toilet open with my phone inside it. She must've smashed it before putting it in there.

Layla was pulling at my shirt while I stood in the bathroom speechless. A minute later, I heard the garage door opening. Before I could get outside, Denise drove off.

Kim

Daddy called me last night and begged us to spend the last couple of days at my parents' house. I didn't want to deal with my mom, but for Ava's sake, I agreed. She could bond a little more with her grandmother before we left for good. The next time I'd see any of them would be in California. It would take years for me to force myself to come back.

Thank God for technology because that's the only form of communication we'd have. One click of a button and I wouldn't have to listen to anyone's unsolicited advice or judgment.

My aunt and I packed up and made the dreaded drive to my parents' house. Daddy behaved strangely when we arrived. We walked into the house and faced my mom in the foyer. She handed me a card in an envelope.

"Kim, I'm sorry about how I acted. I just wanted so much more for your life. You have already done a lot of great things, but sometimes I get caught up in my ways. From now on, I will let you live your life. I will be there to support you in whatever you do and whatever you may go through."

"How many times did you rehearse that with a straight face?" I asked, laughing.

"Kim?" Daddy said from behind me.

I rolled my eyes. The stench of bullshit rose from that apology, but at least she said it. I had to give her that much. It only took a week.

"Sorry. Thank you, Mom. I appreciate it."

"I made you a lemon cake with your grandma's recipe. And with whipped cream icing," she told me.

"Oh, dang. Y'all laying it on thick. I will take it. Let me put our things in the room, and I'll get a slice. Thank you."

"No problem," she said. Mom's eyes lit up when I handed Ava over.

Daddy had already brought the bags in the house, so I helped him take them to the back room. Aunt Vivica followed behind us. I dropped my stuff on the floor and he did the same. Aunt Vivica walked into my room. My dad gave me a look like he wanted to say something.

"What? I said thank you. Daddy, you do realize that wasn't a real apology, right?"

He shook his head. "That's not it."

"What's wrong?"

"I talked to Viv about Brian. She said he came to the hotel for Ava."

"Yeah. Thanks to you."

Daddy tilted his head to the side. Aunt Vivica put up her church finger and walked out.

"I mean, yes. He came over," I corrected myself.

"Mmm. Viv also told me you're moving to California permanently."

"Dang, do I ever get to tell my business before anyone else does?"

"Kim, I thought you initially stayed longer because of Ava's father. Now that he knows, why are you going back?"

"Daddy, I don't want to be here. Not with him, not with Mom when she finds out. I'm sure someone will tell her before I do. It's not the life I want. My daughter's father is married to someone I once called my best friend. Whenever he tells her, I don't know how things will be."

"Baby girl, I hear you. Things are not perfect. You made some huge mistakes to get you where you are right now. My main concern is for that baby of yours. What kind of relationship will she have with her father?"

"Ugh! Have you been talking to Brian too? I don't want to keep fighting everyone. It's my life."

"Now that's where you're wrong. It's Ava's life. Once she came into the picture, the focus is not on your wants anymore but on her needs. Her father is one of them."

"He will always be her father. No matter where we live, nothing will change that, unfortunately. I told him that he'd still see her. He'd have to come to California to do so. I will not be bringing her back and forth."

"Kim, why not stay? Every child needs both of their parents. Sadly, it doesn't always work out that way for everyone, but you have the opportunity to give that to your daughter."

"Oh my goodness! He can still be in her life. Plus, when she's older, I'll let Ava visit all of you for the summers and stuff. That's if his wife would even allow it. I doubt she'd be okay with this although Brian is so sure she will be. I'd rather keep my distance and live in peace."

"Think about your daughter is all I'm asking. As a father, I would *never* want to have a long distance relationship with my young child. I understand that it is an uncomfortable situation, but you can't change it. No matter the despicable actions that brought Ava into this world, she shouldn't suffer without both of her parents. Especially when they will both love her like she deserves. Brian will be a great dad to her."

Dammit. My dad had to play the "your child will suffer for it" card. I didn't want to hurt her in the long run, but I didn't see the point in staying here while she's so little. She wouldn't remember any of this, anyway. Maybe in a couple years. Sure, Brian would adore her as my dad did with us, but I had to consider the quality of our lives and happiness. Selfishly, my joy would be at a higher level far away from this madness.

Our conversation ended since Mom announced that she wanted to cut the cake. Everyone met her in the kitchen. We all sat at the table with our oversized slices and gushed over Ava. Mom told me that my grandparents, my sister, and my brother planned to come over this evening. Since we'd fly back on Monday morning, most of them would be at work.

Less than an hour later, my grandparents arrived. Grandma had a slice of the cake and acted like she sucked a lemon. She told my mom the flavor was too strong, and she didn't like the whipped cream frosting. It tasted perfect to me. Then again, I remembered that we become our moms. Watching them gave me a glimpse into the future. We'd probably be clashing forever. I didn't have the energy to change it at this point.

When my siblings arrived, the party started. My sister brought wine and my brother brought the beer. Grandpa passed Ava onto someone else after he told me to grab him a beer. He'd be asleep soon. My grandfather missed most of the excitement because he was always tired. Yes, he got old but damn. He retired years ago; I didn't know what wore him out every day.

My cousins on my mom's side came over. They were the best cooks in the family and prepared for tonight's fish fry. I helped them in the kitchen for a while before Ava got fussy. After I fed her, I laid her down in our room and came back into the living room.

Someone knocked hard and rang the doorbell. Keisha

answered it. She sounded surprised at whoever came over. Then Denise walked into the living room alone. Her face gave away her knowledge of everything. I recognized it in her eyes.

We had a full house. I feared what she'd say in front of everyone more than what I would have to face alone. Taking her outside to get the verbal bashing was my first choice.

I walked toward her hoping she'd allow me to lead her away from my family's view. As soon as I got close enough, she slapped the hell out of me.

"Oh!" someone said.

"Hey!" my sister yelled as she pulled Denise away.

I held my face. The sting felt like my cheek was growing.

"What the hell?" one of my cousins said.

Mom rushed over and looked like she'd jump on Denise who hadn't spoken a word. Only a few of us understood the motive behind it.

"Have you lost your mind?" Mom asked her while I held my mother back.

"Ask your daughter," Denise countered.

"Mom, it's okay. Dee can we talk outside?"

"Oh, please. I'm not helping yo' hoe ass pretend like you didn't fuck my husband. No! Everyone in here needs to know that this bitch fucked my fucking husband and had his baby."

The gasps and yelps of shock and disbelief came from everyone. Daddy stood in front of me. "Young lady, I want you to get out of here right now. You will not come into my home and disrespect my family like this."

"*Me*? You should tell your lying ass, nasty ass, hoe ass daughter that."

"Now that is enough," he yelled.

Denise looked dead at me with tears falling down to her shirt. "Why, Kim? Why would you do this to me?"

My worst nightmare stared me in the face, and I didn't

have the guts to challenge her. Every word she spoke was true. I wouldn't dare try to deny it.

"I loved you like a sister. How could you? I fucking hate you. You and your stupid daughter," Denise bawled. My dad walked toward her to get her out. "You two can have each other. You can rot in hell, you dirty bitch," she ranted.

Daddy finally got her through the front door and shut it behind them. I heard her yelling from outside. He told her to leave repeatedly.

All eyes focused on me. Mom was in tears standing next to me. She took a few steps back like she'd catch a disease if she got too close. "Please tell me that she is mistaken, Kimberly. You did no such thing."

Aunt Vivica came over and guided me to the hall and forced me into her room. I heard my mom yell, telling everyone to get out. In silence, they all left. I had never known for my family to be so quiet.

My sister came into the room. She sat on the bed next to me while my aunt stood near the dresser. We looked like kids hiding out while our parents calmed down. No one wanted to be the first to break the silence.

Someone knocked on the bedroom door. Aunt Vivica opened it and let Daddy in. He stood beside her and said nothing.

I couldn't take it anymore. I left the room and immediately wished I hadn't. Mom was in the hall facing the door I walked through. I froze.

"Out of all the things you have done, this was the last thing I'd ever think you were capable of," she said, wiping her face. "Kimberly, this is too much. This is unbelievable. It's disgusting and...and...I can't look at you." She brushed past me, then stopped to face me again. "A married man, Kim? Your friend's husband? Where did you come from? No one has ever disgraced this family as much as you have. You should be ashamed of yourself."

Mom went into her room and shut the door. I continued walking until I found myself on the front porch. Minutes later, Keisha came and sat next to me on the bench. She kept quiet for a while. When her hand grabbed and squeezed mine, more tears fell. I didn't know if I was more ashamed of my actions or how Denise told everyone. I leaned on my little sister's shoulder.

"Everything will blow over soon enough," she told me.

"I'm not so sure about that. Now, I will forever be remembered as the woman who got pregnant by her friend's husband."

"Yep, that's about right. You know how the family is. You got that scarlet A now." We laughed. It hurt because of all the crying.

"Man, this is insane. Brian is your baby daddy?"

"Ugh, don't say that."

"Well, it's true so accept hearing it."

"You not mad at me like everyone else?"

"Shit, it wasn't me. So, what do I have to be mad about?"

I nudged her, then sat back up.

"Girl, I almost had to pop a bitch in front of Grandma."

"Ha! Yeah right. You stood there as frozen as I was."

"I was in shock, but in my mind, I swung at her. By the way, does your face hurt?"

"You ain't funny."

She burst out laughing. "Yeah, I bet it doesn't. Denise don't look like she can fight."

"I cannot believe that happened. It felt like everything was in slow motion."

"Damn, girl. Brian?"

"Shut up."

"You did it. You shut up."

Daddy and Aunt Vivica came outside. "You okay, baby girl?" he asked.

"What do you think, Harold? You were there," Aunt Vivica told him.

"What a night, huh?" he asked as if it would lighten the mood.

"The worst one yet," I said.

"We all saw this was coming. I didn't see it coming like it did, but still," Aunt Vivica let out.

Keisha looked at each one of us. "Hold up, Daddy! You knew?"

"Yeah," he answered.

"You too, Auntie?" she asked.

"Mmmhmm," Aunt Viv affirmed.

"So, I'm the only one who didn't," Keisha concluded.

"You and the million people who were in the room," I said.

"Oh, yeah. I'm so sorry that this is happening to you," Keisha stated.

"I'm the one who let it. It is what it is," I replied.

"But Brian? He is cute, but he's so...dorky," Keisha exclaimed in disgust.

"And married," Aunt Vivica blurted.

"Okay, okay. Can we please get off it already?" I asked.

"You should've never gotten on it," Aunt Vivica said under her breath.

"Eww," Keisha whined.

"Let me go check on your mother. Kim, do not make any rash decisions because of this. I still meant what I said earlier. Think about Ava. Before you say anything, your mother will get over this. It has nothing to do with her. She will live," Daddy stated before he gave Keisha and me a kiss on our foreheads.

My aunt and sister tried to change the subject. I couldn't

keep up with whatever they were talking about. Brian must have been dead somewhere. He hadn't called to tell me he broke his word. His loyalty was to his wife as it should be, but damn he could've given me a heads up.

Everything felt surreal. This would definitely be my last visit to Houston. The dust that flew up today would take years to settle, and I was willing to wait even longer. I was done with Houston and wanted to leave my sins behind with it.

# Brian

BRIAN

The delivery guy handed me my sub sandwich. It had been the third time this week he brought dinner to my door. Denise left me over a month ago. I was recovering from the chaos of my life. She was in charge of our house and without her, everything was out of order.

Denise turned off my cell phone and didn't pay any of our bills. My mom and I searched the place for the accounts notebook that had all the logins and passwords, but we couldn't find it. I didn't even know who we paid for what service. The only solution was to wait until I got a late bill and change the info from there. I hadn't gotten it all straightened out yet.

My wife dropped me and everything else and moved to Atlanta with her parents who now hated me as much as she did. I used to have a close relationship with her dad.

The two women who had my children put their anger and disgust for me ahead of the girls. It wasn't fair. Kim left Houston without telling me. When I called her to visit Ava before their flight, she was already in California. That's when I found out that Denise confronted her.

On that night, Denise came into the house pissed. I assumed she left for a long drive, not to slap Kim in front of her family. I should've listened to her about everything.

My wife said less than ten words to me after I told her what I had done. The following week, she moved out when I left for work. I came home to an empty house. No letter, no text on my new phone. Nothing.

At least Kim talked to me again after I broke my promise. We couldn't have prepared for the outcome, but it never dawned on me how unpredictable my wife would become. I no longer recognized the woman I spent the last nine years with.

Kim let me see Ava on video chat, and we planned for me to visit them this weekend. I needed my daughters. Even if I could only be around one of them, I'd take it. Denise had more to be angry about, so I intended to give her time.

I only wished she'd let me be there for Layla. It killed me being away from my baby girl. A month was a long time. I bet she grew a lot. Denise stopped all communication, and I feared she'd file for divorce.

Friday, after work, I caught a cab to the airport and got on a plane. It was a painful flight. When left to my thoughts, they tortured me. All my fears played out much worse than I imagined. I assumed things would get bad, but not this bad. One slip up and I was being punished by abandonment.

I never wanted to be like my father, yet that path laid right in front of me. I was determined to create another one so my kids won't grow up like I did. Whatever I needed to do, it would get done to the best of my ability. I'd die before I'd turn into that man.

That man left my mom and me and started a family with another woman. Those kids got the father I wished I had, but the same blood flowed through us. I feared Ava would experience something similar since her mother was the other woman.

Now, I faced this possibility with both of my children. Things were more complicated in my case, but in their eyes, the only thing that counted was my absence. I had to fix it before they got old enough to notice.

I didn't want my girls to ever feel I didn't love them, but being kept from Layla gave me no options to prove myself to her. I prayed that Denise would soon give me a chance to be the best father I could be even if she chooses to never forgive me.

When the plane landed, I caught another cab to get to the address that Kim gave me. The ride took forever. We went through the security gate and found the house. I knocked on the door and when it opened; I saw one of the most beautiful faces on the planet.

Ava had gotten so big in such a short time. Kim nodded before handing Ava over. It was strange that she wouldn't hug me anymore. Her aunt spoke and asked about the flight. She welcomed me with more enthusiasm than the mother of my child.

Kim showed me to my room where I put my things down and followed her to the nursery. I was floored at how beautiful this house looked. Not only the size but the decor and the layout.

I felt like a stranger which was kind of true. Even though I had known Kim longer than I did Denise, our friendship changed when we crossed that line the second time. Any time we talked, we argued. She wouldn't budge on staying in California.

I threatened to fight her for custody a couple weeks ago. That proved to be the wrong move. I wasn't serious, but I wanted Kim to know I had rights too.

Once Kim spoke to me again, I begged her to let me see

Ava in person. She banished herself from Houston, so this was my best bet to spend time with my daughter.

Most of my first day I talked with her aunt. Kim took Ava to breastfeed her and then brought her back if she hadn't fallen asleep. She allowed me to change Ava's diaper a couple times and even pumped milk for me to feed her.

It was crazy that the woman I could never be with treated me better than my wife. Sometimes, I wondered what would've happened if I had married Kim instead.

For starters, the mess we had created wouldn't exist since she'd be the only one. I didn't regret marrying Denise because of anything she did, but I should've broken things off after the first time I slept with Kim. The fact that fate pulled us together back then proved I should've chosen her.

Even then, I tried to do the right thing and hurting Denise didn't feel like the move to make. If I had, there would've been far less collateral damage. Now, I had to awkwardly be around Kim who I wrongfully shared a child with.

All of it sounded horrible in theory, but I didn't regret Ava for one second. I still loved her mother. If things went all the way wrong with Denise and she divorced me, I'd hope that Kim and I could be closer. She would not be with me in the capacity I'd dream of, but maybe I'd get my friend back.

At dinner, she opened up a bit. Her aunt poured each of us a glass of wine. Kim asked about Layla and if I had seen her. I didn't divulge the state of my relationship with Denise before. Our previous conversations were only related to Ava.

I told her the truth and admitted she was right about my wife turning into someone I didn't know she could be. Kim seemed sympathetic and blamed herself. I let her know I didn't blame her for any of it.

After we finished, Vivica suggested we go to the balcony while she cleaned the kitchen. Kim offered to help her, but she wouldn't let her.

We went outside, and I fell in love with the view. It was mesmerizing. Kim shared that this was where she spent most of her alone time when the weather allowed it. I could see why. The set up out here was welcoming. There was enough furniture outside to fill a studio apartment.

"Kim, I'm sorry for how things transpired. I know I said it before, but we weren't in person, and I don't think you believe that none of it was on purpose."

"I believed you the first time."

"Then why are you so quiet around me?"

"I don't know. Everything is confusing now. I mean, we have a child together. It doesn't even sound right saying it out loud."

"Yeah, you're right about that. But do you forgive me for... hell, for all of this?"

"Yes, Brian. You were in a bad spot having to keep such a secret from Denise. I am sorry for how things are going. I hoped I was wrong about how she'd take it. If I put myself in her shoes, it's obvious why she is distancing herself. She's enraged and devastated. It would be too hard for her to look at you. I didn't think she'd keep the baby from you though."

"You and me both. I think that's been the hardest part. Denise has every right to despise me, but not being able to hold or talk to Layla is the ultimate punishment. That's why I'm so grateful you let me come here."

"Well, you can thank my dad for that. When you threatened to file for custody, I almost lost it."

"Hey, I'm sorry about that too. I only wanted to give you a reason to move back to Houston. It was a stupid and insensitive way to scare you into it."

"Mmm."

I looked down at the glass of wine in my hand. It got so quiet that we heard Vivica cleaning in the kitchen.

"Kim?"

"Yeah."

"Look at me." She did. "I will never ever do anything like that to you. You are a remarkable mother, and I trust you have Ava's best interest at heart. I would never take her away from you."

"I appreciate that. Don't be so sure you would've won. I'd fight dirty if I needed to. Nobody will make me move back there."

We laughed. Kim made Houston sound like an undesirable country she ran from.

"It's not that bad."

"Um, did you forget that your wife ran up in my parents' house with everyone there? She came in there talking about 'you fucked my husband' and 'hoe ass this and that.' I won't ever be able to face any of them again. My mom won't talk to me at all. When I Skype with my dad, my aunt has to get on the call with Ava for my mom to see her. She wants nothing to do with me. It's been over a month."

"Damn."

"Damn indeed. One night changed everything. This is why I *love* keeping my secrets," she said, imitating me.

"Ooh. You remember that?"

"That shit hurt my feelings."

"I'm sorry."

We sat outside for over an hour. I tried to convince Kim to move to Houston with a promise to keep her from Denise if my wife ever came back. The fact that I'd be a steady presence in Ava's life wasn't a hard enough sell. She said she needed time to get to a place where she'd even consider it.

We agreed to come back to this option in a year. It should be plenty of time for things to cool down and for Kim to be comfortable living so close to her family. I didn't believe anyone would be as hard on her as she feared. Then again, I didn't have a good track record with assuming how anyone would take things.

The morning of my flight back home, Ms. Vivica booked a photographer for a session at her house.

Ava and I took pictures together and then Ava and her mom. The photographer asked if we wanted any together. Kim declined.

Her aunt pushed for us to do it so Ava would have pictures of her whole family. Kim said those types of photos would be lying to our daughter about the state of our relationship. Ms. Vivica persuaded us to take them anyway. Kim told me I would not get copies of those photos. I concurred that it wouldn't be a good look if they got in the wrong hands.

♬♬♬

At home alone, I had a lot of time to reflect on my life and the decisions I'd made. Love caused my problems. I didn't know how to turn it off. My feelings for both Kim and Denise conflicted me. My wife was my priority, but she completely pushed me to the side.

On the other hand, I'd been visiting with Ava so often that Kim and I were talking as friends again. She showed me the love I desperately desired, and it made me feel some kind of way. The same feelings that got me into this chaos. I wouldn't act on them but seeing her so happy around me complicated things.

After three months of only seeing Ava, Denise responded to a text and sent me one picture of Layla. I cried. My baby was growing up without me. Four pop up visits to Atlanta, and she denied me access to my daughter each time.

On my last try, her dad contacted me. He claimed he only did what Denise asked of him although he now disagreed with her. Even if I lost my wife over this, her dad agreed I shouldn't be separated from Layla. In time, I prayed he'd get through to her on my behalf. I wanted my daughter.

ᆏᆏᆏ

LAYLA's first birthday was coming in a week. I asked Denise if I could be there for it, but she didn't respond. I figured that I'd at least try so my flight would get me there the night before. That didn't work. So, I left Layla's birthday gifts with her granddad and returned home defeated.

My father-in-law and I texted over the last couple weeks. Her dad sent me a video of Layla walking around their house. It broke my heart. Even though Denise's dad respected her wishes and kept me from the house, he made a deal with me. If I said nothing, he'd bring Layla to my hotel whenever I came.

Since Denise banned me from the party, I was eternally grateful that her dad gave me this opportunity. For one hour, he allowed me to spend time with my daughter. I didn't even think she'd remember me.

When I put my hands out to take her from her grandfather, she reached out for me. I wrapped my arms around my baby and held her tight. My vision blurred from all the tears. I missed my little girl.

When it was time for them to leave, her dad apologized that Layla got caught up in our situation. He recognized that keeping her from me was harsh since it had been almost five months. It made life hard.

Work annoyed me, my family couldn't help, and being in that empty house drove me insane. Kim somewhat filled that void, but she was all the way in California. I couldn't see Ava in person whenever.

Although I appreciated seeing her through my phone every night. It was still hard not being the type of dad I wanted to be for either of my girls.

WE HAD AVA'S NINE-MONTH CHECKUP TODAY WITH Dr. FineAssHell. I looked forward to seeing him. That type of eye candy satisfied my daydreams. My imagination would get a dose to hold me over.

Brian stayed on my mind since we talked every day. It confused the hell out of me. Then I realized that I loved him. His relationship with Ava made my feelings harder to deny.

Dr. Thomas helped suppress those feelings temporarily. When he came into the room, he wore a smile that teased my soul and other body parts. I'd usually use Ava as a distraction, but today my plan failed. I caught myself staring a few times.

After the exam, he sat across from me explaining that she was all good and asked if I had questions. I told him no.

Dr. Fine fidgeted in his chair for a few moments and kept clearing his throat. I felt like he was stalling or something, which made me nervous.

"Is there a problem, Dr. Thomas?"

"Sort of," he answered.

"Oh my God! Is something wrong with my daughter?"

"No, no. Ava's great. Perfect health," he assured me.

"So, what is it?"

"Miss Duncan."

"Kim is fine."

"Okay, Kim. You can call me Evan." He smiled and straightened his shirt. "This may be an odd request, and I am sorry for the inconvenience."

"What inconvenience?" I asked.

Evan cleared his throat. "To be honest, I'm attracted to you. My feelings are highly inappropriate which is why you should consider finding another doctor for Ava."

He looked so serious, but this had to be a joke. I laughed. "You're kidding, right? Who put you up to this?"

"Um, no one."

"Yeah right. Was it Marissa? Marissa Rice? Whatever she said to you is not true."

"Kim, I have no idea who that is."

"So, you can't be Ava's doctor because of me?"

"Yes."

"Wow."

"This is strange, I'm sure. There's something about you and I—"

"You don't have to explain yourself. I would've done the same thing sooner or later."

"Oh?"

"Yeah. I call you Dr. Fine to other people." I put my hand over my mouth. He chuckled. "You didn't hear me say that."

Evan glanced at Ava. "How does Ava get along with her dad?"

I poked my lips out to the side. "If you're asking if he's in the picture, yes. But only for her. We are not together."

"Oh, really?" he asked with a smirk.

"You don't have to sound so happy."

"Sorry, I um...Would you like to have lunch or something?"

"Does that mean I'd still have to get a new doctor?"

"Whether you say yes or no, you should. The latter would be somewhat embarrassing for us if you had to deal with me again."

"True. What the heck? Let's do it. Well, not it, it. I mean, yes." I dropped my head as he got out a good laugh.

His smile burned into my memory. What the hell was I doing? Then again, one date couldn't hurt.

"You can refer me to someone. Preferably a woman."

Even his laughs sounded sexy. Something had to be wrong with him.

ᛈᛈᛈ

THE FOLLOWING WEEK, Evan and I planned a walk in the park near my aunt's house. I brought Ava along in case he got the wrong impression from the other day. I didn't realize he'd make a picnic.

Evan impressed me. We walked and talked for about fifteen minutes before finding a good spot to sit. I took Ava from her stroller and put her down on the blanket Evan laid on the ground. She immediately crawled to him.

"Looks like one of you likes me," he said.

Seeing her with him and how his eyes gleamed was uneasy. Clearly, he loved kids based on his profession, but this felt different.

Since he was busy with Ava, I opened the basket. He packed fruit, cheese, crackers, and mini sub sandwiches. The half cheesecake got me excited. I pulled everything out onto the blanket.

"Did you make all of this yourself?" I asked.

"I sure did."

"Look at you!"

"My mother taught me how to cook. She always said I

might find a wife that couldn't."

We laughed.

"Smart woman. A lot of the women in my family cooked, so I don't have that problem. I've met many women who claimed that cooking was beneath them though."

"I dated a few of them. Although my mother prepared me, she had a hard time liking any woman who didn't."

He grinned until Ava grabbed his face. Then he looked down at her asking her what kind of things I've said about him.

"She is a mommy's girl. You will get nothing out of her."

"I bet."

Evan sat with her in his lap the whole time, and she didn't want me to get her. She didn't know this man. Neither did I.

While we talked, he attended to her. He even peeled grapes and sliced them with a plastic knife. Evan explained how grapes were dangerous for little kids, but they loved eating them. I didn't give them to her at all. It was too much work, but not for him I guess.

We talked about the basics at first. Evan was born in Arizona and moved to California after he divorced his wife. When I asked why, he explained that she had a baby with a close family friend. The wind was knocked out of me. This great guy was the Denise in his situation. No way we'd move past this date.

After we ate, I confessed everything about what I had done to bring Ava here. He pulled at his shirt collar and swallowed hard. The constant eye contact was no more. I felt ashamed, but the truth was the truth. I didn't want to end up falling for him and then have to tell my story. I had to rip off the band-aid.

The walk back to our cars was quiet. I told him that I wouldn't blame him for never wanting to see me again. All I got from him was "get home safe."

What happened to him was messed up, and the similarity to my situation didn't help. Trying to force anyone to accept my past wasn't something I ever planned on doing. If the truth was too much to handle, we would not work out. One night with Brian would be a stain I'd wear because of Ava.

Days later, Evan still hadn't called. I scared him off, and he had every right not to trust me. Not that it was an accurate judgment of my character.

Aunt Vivica was surprised that I told Evan the truth since I was adamant on keeping my secret not too long ago.

BRIAN SCHEDULED a trip here next week. He informed me that Denise still hadn't talked to him. If anyone deserved forgiveness, he did. Brian tried so hard to prove himself to at least visit his daughter. Not wanting anything to do with Brian or me was one thing but holding Layla hostage was the worst pain she could inflict on him. He was a great father and loved his kids.

The guilt for my part made me consider moving to Houston so he could be with Ava more often. I had nothing keeping me in California, and I grew tired of hiding out. I missed my dad and sister and brother. Ava needed them too. My family wasn't able to visit as much as Brian did.

We spent time together with some normalcy. Brian left his issues at the door every time he saw Ava. The love in his eyes said so. It was heartwarming to witness the love he had for her.

Ava took a lot of steps in the past week. I sent a video to him when she took her first steps, but to watch her walk in person made him cry. Brian was extremely emotional these days. I wanted to make sure he was a part of everything Ava did since he had missed them all with Layla.

At one point he claimed he would file for divorce and joint

custody. He convinced himself that Denise would never forgive him and the only way he'd be in Layla's life was through the court system. I advised him to give Denise a little more time, but I'd support him either way.

On Brian's second night, we were home alone with Ava. Aunt Vivica stayed over her son's house. Marissa and Cory wanted a date night, so she babysat while they went out on the town. She was an incredible grandmother. Those were some lucky kids.

We rented an animated movie and chilled with Ava for most of the evening. Brian kept giving me this look that I didn't like. I got up from the couch to get a bottle of water. When I closed the refrigerator, he was standing behind me.

"What are you doing?" I asked.

I looked past him to the living room where Ava was asleep on the couch, mouth open, and everything.

"Can I ask you something?"

I walked around him and sat on a bar stool. "Sure."

"Do you ever wonder about us?"

"Is that why you keep giving me those bedroom eyes?"

"What? No, I'm not."

"Yes, you are. And I noticed you looking at my ass."

He laughed. "You're the one walking around in those pants. You know what you're doing."

"Boy, please. These are comfortable."

"Sure they are. But you didn't answer my question."

"I don't need to. The only reason you are asking me that is because Denise is still mad. Be patient."

"What's the point? She won't ever take me back. Why can't we—"

"Stop, Brian. Don't even go there. We can't because it's wrong. It was wrong then and still is. All we can do is let that little girl know how loved she is."

"Kim, I loved you first. We can start over the right way this time."

"In what world, Brian? That is not in the cards for us."

"You're wrong. If it wasn't, we wouldn't have Ava. She was meant to be here the same way we belong together. You can't lie and say you feel nothing for me."

"Yes, I love you. You are the father of my child. We will be connected forever through her, and that's it."

"Why? Why can't we stop acting like we don't know what this is?"

"Boy, what are you talking about?"

"Us! This! That night in college and the night that made us parents. I made the mistake of not choosing you the first time, and I am paying the price with Layla. What's stopping us from doing the right thing?"

"The right thing is for you to fight for your wife and continue being a great father to your daughters."

Brian walked over to my chair and put his hands on my shoulders. A tingle flowed through my body. "Kim, I love you, and now that I have another chance, I don't want to miss out." He wrapped his arms around me from behind.

My body was acting dumb as hell. It should know better than to allow his touches to feel so good. I stood up to move from his grasp, but he blocked me with an arm on each side of me. "No, we are not doing this again. Brian snap out of it. You are still married."

He picked me up and sat me on the large island. "Don't you want me? I can't stop thinking about you."

"I don't," I lied.

He slid his hands under my shirt, and I pushed them out.

"Think about what you're doing. Think about Layla. If we do this, Denise will never allow you around her."

He smacked his lips and leaned in. The tip of his nose

touched my cheek. I kept my head down. Brian put his hand under my chin and made me look up at him.

"No," I whispered.

"Yes," he said before kissing me.

"No," I moaned.

Even my body ignored my voice. My panties moistened as his tongue twirled with mine. He squeezed my ass and pulled me off of the island. I wrapped my legs around his waist without breaking away from his lips.

Brian slid his hand into my pants and got too close to that wet spot. I jumped down.

"We can't," I whined, pulling away from him.

"Yes, we can. It's not like we haven't before," he replied, getting annoyed.

"Listen to yourself. We can't keep doing this."

I walked to the other side of the island to keep a safe distance.

"Kim, stop fighting it. Just be with me. We can deal with the rest of the stuff together."

"Brian, no. I don't want this."

"It didn't feel that way a minute ago."

"Because you're confusing me. My body not listening doesn't count. This is still wrong no matter how we feel."

"You said yourself that you chose me. I was the stupid one back then. But everything is so clear now. Choose me again."

"No, Brian. College was college. It was too long ago to matter anymore. I only confessed that stuff to you because I was upset. It didn't mean anything. Besides, everything has changed. You know we cannot do this. Not now, not ever again."

He pulled back a chair at the bar and sat down with his elbows propped on the countertop.

"I don't know what I know anymore. My wife left me. Everything fucking sucks back home. I have no one there with me. She's never coming back. I screwed that up for good. We did. I do know that I've always loved you. Why can't we just be a family? Hell, I'd even move to California."

I didn't want to hurt him even more. Brian pulled at my heart and excited the places in my body that he shouldn't. The way he looked at me and how his touches tempted me to give in. All this shit about connections and destiny almost seemed true, but I won't succumb to it. He was my friend, and we were getting too close because of Ava.

I accepted our relationship as simply friends years ago, and I wanted to keep it that way. The sexual attraction blinded the both of us more than once. We were adults, not some horny teens. If we keep this up, these visits would have to stop for a while. We both needed space to clear our heads.

"Brian, I won't lie and say I don't care for you. But we must be responsible. Our mistake brought Ava into this world, and we can't take that back. However, you have a beautiful family apart from us. That is not something you'd want to throw away. Fix your relationship with your wife and stop trying to start one with me. The fact that we love each other will never be enough to ignore that you chose to spend your life with Denise. You guys have something special. You still love her as you should. Don't let this setback cause you to dig a deeper hole for yourself."

"What am I supposed to do?" he asked.

"Be strong and keep fighting for her, not me. We have to accept the truth about us. We cannot be together the way you want. It will never be right."

He put his head down for a few moments. Then he stared into my eyes. "I'm sorry. I'm all over the place, and I can't discern which path to take. You and Ava mean so much to me, but you're right. I still love my wife. The way she's acting infuriates me and makes me feel unwanted. Then I come here, and the woman I wanted for so long accepts me with open arms. I didn't intend on doing this to you. I'm really sorry. You trusted me, and now I'm messing things up."

"We're good. Life is hard for you right now, and I don't want to make it worse. I will always be a part of you and you of me, but we can only be Ava's parents. And friends, of course. Well maybe until your wife comes back. I'm sure she'd want you to have nothing to do with me."

"Like that will ever happen. She's done with me, and no one will ever keep me from you and Ava. You guys are my family too."

Brian smiled with much pain in his eyes. I hated to watch him in this position. I wished I could give him what he wanted, but I wouldn't be able to live with myself. This was for the best, no matter if my heart felt differently.

We called it a night. I let Ava sleep in the room with him. This way he would focus his attention on his daughter and not me.

Ava woke up before Brian, so I tip-toed into his room to get her. She giggled a little too loud when I picked her up from her bassinet. Brian caught us leaving. He apologized for last night and offered to make breakfast. By the end of his attempt, we had to air out the house. He took us out to eat instead.

We went to a restaurant in Richmond with great reviews. When we placed our order, my phone rang a few times before I found it in my purse. Evan's name appeared on the screen. My heart raced. What did he want?

I excused myself and took the call outside. He claimed that he needed time to digest what I told him concerning Ava's conception.

"Kim, there is something about you that I can't shake and as hard as it was to hear your truth, I still can't get you off my mind."

"Um, I'm sorry? Kind of. Not really."

He laughed. "Can we get together soon? I want to ask you

some things."

"Um, sure. I'm out right now."

"Me too. I'm walking to my favorite breakfast spot since I can't think clearly enough to cook for myself."

"Damn, it's that bad?" He didn't answer.

After moments of silence, he asked, "What do you have on?"

"Say what?"

"No, no!" he said. I heard him laugh. It was loud enough to echo. "That didn't come out right. I think I see you. Look up." He waved from the streetlight, waiting to cross.

"Oh, wow. I hope you're not stalking me, Dr. Thomas."

"Don't worry. I'm not that crazy."

Evan walked toward me as we hung up. We hugged. I explained that I was having breakfast with Ava and her father.

"Good thing he burned breakfast, huh?"

"Yeah, I guess it is. He's actually what I wanted to talk to you about."

"Really?"

"Look, Kim. I like you, and I know we hadn't spent much time together, but I hoped that we could. What you told me the other day threw me."

"I thought it would. I did an awful thing, and I know it's a turnoff. My actions then don't define who I am every day, but I can see how it can ruin anyone's perception of me. It's something I will have to deal with."

"That's the thing. I still want to see you because I understand that things happen. I forgave my wife for it even though I can't be with her. We don't know each other that well but I would like to learn more about who you are now."

"Really?"

"Yes, but I have a few questions first."

"Okay, shoot."

"Are you in love with Ava's dad?"

"I don't know. I mean, I do love him, but not so much in love if that makes any sense."

"Well, is there any chance that you would go back to him?"

"Not at all. We were never together."

"So, if we did this, and it worked out, he wouldn't be a threat?"

"Not at all. You can meet him now if you want to find out."

"Maybe later."

"He's a friend who happens to be the father of my baby. Nothing more."

"Okay. Should I worry about you not being faithful? Is that something you struggled with in the past?"

"I never cheated on my ex. We were together for eight years, and it was only him. He did the cheating in that relationship. It should never be a concern."

"Are you sure? I want to be clear on what I expect and what I want to avoid."

"I appreciate you being upfront about your concerns. Usually, guys assume the worst and go from there. I do hope that I can prove what I am telling you."

"Me too."

We agreed to plan a date soon. I didn't want to keep Brian waiting. Evan gave me another hug before we realized he was going into the same restaurant. I asked him to sit with us, but he declined and sat at the counter.

When I returned to our table, Brian stared at me. He asked about Evan since he saw us talking outside and walk in together. I told him the truth. The first thing he thought was that Evan was the reason for me not trying to get with him. He had no place being jealous. Brian had to make amends with his wife, and I should move on with my life. Evan was the first step.

# Denise

"DEE?" MOMMA CALLED.

"Ma'am?"

"Come in here and eat lunch with me."

"No thank you, Momma. I'm not hungry."

"Girl, don't you start that again. You need to eat," she yelled from the other side of the house.

If I wanted any peace, I'd have to do what she says. That woman was a pushy one, and I didn't have the will to push back.

When I walked into the kitchen, she stood near the sink washing the few dishes inside.

"There you are, beautiful. Come on, you gotta taste this," Momma said, sliding a bowl toward me when I sat at the table.

I lowered my face to the bowl to get a whiff. "What is it?"

"Turkey salad. Just like Nana's."

"Where is she? Shouldn't she be the judge?" I asked, trying to get out of eating it.

"Rita took her to a doctor appointment," she explained while opening a cookie jar to get crackers.

Momma sat down next to me and moved the bowl between us. She put a spoonful of salad onto a cracker.

"Taste it." She held the cracker near my mouth.

I turned away. "I don't want to."

"What, you got a problem with my cooking?"

"Yep, that's it. I hate your cooking." She bumped my shoulder with hers. I exhaled slowly. "I'm not in the mood to eat today."

My mother put the cracker down. Layla and my dad were at the neighborhood park, so I had no way out with a good excuse. I felt like I was on suicide watch some days.

The love and support got me through each day when I needed it. Today was not one of those days. I wanted to be alone and rest my body and mind. To everyone else that meant I was spiraling into depression or something.

"Is it because today's your wedding anniversary?" she asked, placing her hand on mine.

"Momma, I—"

"It's okay, baby. I understand. Take all the time you need."

"Thank you."

"Meanwhile, I'll put a hit out on Brian and have his head delivered as my gift to you."

We laughed. Every time Momma mentioned something like that, it caught me off guard. I loved that woman. She always said the right words and gave me what I needed before I recognized the need. I could not have gotten through these months without her constant attempts to put a smile on my face.

Layla and I moved to Atlanta five months ago, and it had been a journey. When I first arrived, my excuse was I wanted to surprise them, and they were. After a week, the questions poured in. I wouldn't talk about my husband or give them a date of my return to Houston. By the end of the second week, I told my parents everything.

Later that day, my Aunt Rita and cousin Bam came over ready for war. Bam walked into my room where I stayed most of the days.

"So, when are we going to the H?"

"Never," I mumbled.

"Oh, hell naw. We going back. I'm gonna snatch that bitch by the hair and drag her all up and down the streets. She's going to wish she was dead when I'm finished with her. Then I'm gonna bust through your house and pistol whip yo' punk ass, cheating ass husband. Oh, we going."

All her gestures while pacing the floor explaining her plans cheered me up. I would love for her to do those things, and if she had the opportunity, she would. If I ever even thought about moving back, I would not tell Bam. She'd try to go with me and follow through with her threats.

Bam got it from her mom, my Aunt Rita. They were two firecrackers waiting for the chance to go off.

My aunt checked on me in a calmer fashion than her daughter. She understood my low profile, mostly quiet personality. So, that's how she approached me at first. It didn't take long before she threatened Brian's life as well. Our experiences were similar when it came to our husbands.

Aunt Rita was divorced because Uncle Lee slept with half the block when she worked nights. Once she found out, Uncle Lee caught a bullet in his foot.

The way my aunt told the story, my uncle refused to leave when she tried to kick him out. She pulled out her gun, but he still didn't budge, claiming it was his house. Aunt Rita aimed and shot his foot. If he still wouldn't go, she planned on blowing his manhood to pieces. Luckily, being shot once was enough. No charges were filed because Uncle Lee told the first responders that he shot himself by accident.

Aunt Rita had more restraint than me. I wanted to kill

Brian initially. The anger spiraled into sadness that kept me in bed. Thank goodness my parents took over with Layla.

She had to switch to formula because I didn't produce enough breast milk. Not eating enough caused a drought, but Layla transitioned well.

The first month passed, and I still couldn't find the energy to get out of bed. Momma invited her friend over, who happened to be a licensed therapist.

Ms. Carla was lovely, but I didn't want to talk. Both of them were persistent even in my denial of depression. I explained to them multiple times that I was pissed, hurt, and sad at what my husband and best friend had done. All I wanted was time to process things. They gave me space for two weeks until I warmed up to meeting with Ms. Carla.

She came over for Sunday dinners and afterward, we'd talk on the porch or during a walk in the nearby park. I didn't feel analyzed or judged. Ms. Carla treated me like a friend, and she'd share her personal struggles in life as well. No one tried to drug me or label me, we just talked.

With the second month behind me, mornings were easier. I got back to work online and even opened emails I hadn't checked since I got there. I couldn't do anything but laugh. Mountains of emails in my inbox displayed late notices or cancellations of accounts back home. It was a mess. Brian must've had a hard time figuring all of that out, and it made my day.

Brian called and texted often, and I ignored each one. He kept whining about missing Layla. Oh, well. He even had the nerve to show up at my parents' house. I'd have my dad handle him and be done with it. After his third attempt, I almost cared since he tried so hard. Then I'd think of him and Kim together and shut it all down. His ass wouldn't come near me or my baby again.

Today was difficult. I was supposed to be celebrating my

marriage to this once perfect man. Now, I was reminded of how imperfect he was. We all had our faults and challenges, but his were too much to bear. If he'd done what he did with a stranger, things would be different.

I still would've been hurt and upset and may have come to my parents. It may have been easier to face him or let Layla see him. But that wasn't the case. The man I gave my everything to fucked the woman I shared everything with. I had no intentions on ever sharing my husband, but it happened.

Kim betrayed me the most. She introduced me to Brian and raved about this great guy that would be perfect for me. Maybe she wanted him back then too. She probably kept him close by pushing him on me.

Trent was her bad boy, and once he was finished dogging her, she'd come back for the good one she had on standby with me. It was hard to believe since she pretended to love me, but how else could this have happened if she didn't plan it? Brian was a stupid man like the rest of them, but Kim knew what she was doing. I hope that bitch pays for it in this lifetime and the next.

Layla ruled my world. Her smile, her giggle, the way she curled her mouth when she ate solid food, and every single moment of my baby's life. This little girl was the heart of this house as she ran each adult in it.

Nana was Layla's best friend. Thank God her life was spared because she almost missed out on my angel. Nana didn't go a day without sitting out on the porch in the afternoon with Layla. They'd rock on the rocking bench as Nana talked to Layla like she was another adult. Layla loved it. She'd lay her head somewhere on Nana and listen peacefully.

My dad gave me breaks on Saturdays and would take Layla out all day doing whatever. Mom, Aunt Rita, Bam, and I used that time to go shopping or catch a movie. Life was good again although things were still in limbo with Brian. My family inquired on my plans with him. I had no answers. I wanted to ignore him and move on.

Aunt Rita told me to either talk to him or get a divorce. She hated loose ends and uncertainty. It's not like she had to deal with any of it, but she wanted me to have clarity in my life. I agreed to weigh my options. Divorce was the only one that made any sense. It felt too final though. I hadn't seen or spoken to my husband in almost six months.

The pop-up visits were a sign that he cared to fight for us even when he was denied. However, lately, he stopped coming and didn't call as much. I got a few texts about Layla, but that's it. It's almost like he moved on without us.

I joined my dad on his evening stroll after dinner. Locking myself in my room all day didn't help much. Fresh air was the next best thing.

"How you doing, Pumpkin?" Dad asked, leading me to his usual trail.

"I don't know."

"You look horrible."

I pushed him. "Whatever."

"Sweetheart, it's okay to be sad on a day like this with everything you've been through."

"Why did this have to happen? I did everything right. Now, I'm suffering more than him."

"I doubt it."

I looked at him, but he watched the trail. "How? Brian did this to me."

"True, but that doesn't mean he is happy about it."

"Who's side are you on? He's the one who—"

"Forget about what he did for a moment. He was wrong, and I believe he knows it. I'm talking about Layla. His suffering may have a different cause, but he is in pain. I am sure of it."

I stopped walking. How dare my dad sympathize with Brian. "Have you been talking to him?"

"Look, I am disappointed in his actions. But the boy had been a part of this family for years."

"So!"

"So, I care when he wants to be a father to his daughter. I care when I see a man broken down because he has a good heart."

I told my dad and the rest of my family to stay away from Brian. They loved him like a son, but his betrayal to their actual daughter should matter more.

"I cannot believe you."

"Pumpkin, don't get all riled up. I am a father. Am I a good one?"

"Yes, but—"

"Did I make a difference being present in your life?"

"Of course, you did. It still doesn't—"

"Then why can't you let your daughter have the same? How would your life have been if your mother kept you away from me?"

He faced me and placed his hands on my shoulders. "Don't be mad at me for being honest. I think you are too hard on him. Not for what he's done to you, but regarding the man begging to be with his daughter. Layla had nothing to do with the grown-up business. She deserves her father just as much as you did. He's a good man, Denise. A flawed one, but still good."

"Unbelievable! You said you wouldn't go there again. We already talked about this. I don't want him around me right now."

"Like I said before, it's not about you. Let the man see his daughter. She's all he has. I fear he might go off the deep end if you don't give him that much."

"The deep end?"

"I talked to him, and he sounds worse than you did when you first got here. As much as I love you, if I couldn't be around you, or talk to you, or hear your voice at Layla's age, I can't say what I would've done. Men need to know they matter, Denise. Even if only to the innocent babies, he needs something to live for. Someone to work hard for, or else."

"Or else what?"

"He won't have a reason to keep breathing."

"Oh, please. Brian wouldn't hurt himself."

"How do you know? Have you seen him? Do you realize what his mistake and losing you has done to him?"

"I don't care." I walked back the way we came. This time with my dad was supposed to be refreshing. He ruined it for me.

"I am not trying to upset you, Pumpkin. I only want what's best for Layla."

"And for your new best friend."

"I understand you're mad at me for talking to Brian, but think about what I said. Put Layla first."

"I do every single day, Dad."

We said nothing else on the walk back to the house. Momma already put Layla to bed. One glance at my face and she offered me a glass of wine. I took her up on it and ignored my dad for the rest of the night. She asked him about it, but he didn't tell her. Well, at least not in my presence.

My dad finished a beer and went to my parents' room. Momma and I cracked up on reruns of *Golden Girls* for a couple hours before going to bed.

In my room, I watched my beautiful angel sleep. Why did she have to look so much like her dad? All the good times we had were buried under that one night that destroyed my life. I wasn't selfish and didn't want to rob my daughter of a relationship with Brian, but it wasn't so simple.

Our wedding day flashed in my mind and the way he made

me feel each and every day afterward. The places we'd gone. Then I thought of Kim. We spent so much time with her and Trent that this all should've been impossible. She was my number two after Brian. I told her everything, did so much with her, had too many good times to count. I couldn't forgive either of them. If I never saw them again, I wouldn't complain.

Dad had to make me feel guilty. I didn't create this mess. Even though I hated my husband, I didn't want him to hurt himself. I wanted to check if my dad was lying, but I refused to open that door. Brian might get the wrong idea and assume I gave a damn about him.

If I texted him a picture of Layla or something, would that be enough? I didn't want to talk to him. Maybe I should call. That way I'd hear how his voice sounded.

The night Brian told me he cheated replayed in my mind and the same emotions took over. If I couldn't even think about it without getting pissed, how would I let him back into our lives? He did this to us.

# Brian

Sitting in this empty house all week was the misery of my life. It had gotten easier at work since the office was busy. At first, I feared losing my job due to a lack of concentration and a couple of missed deadlines.

Kim helped me get back on track because of Ava. She even came to Houston last weekend, so I wouldn't have to travel this time. She also wanted to see some of her family members.

I offered her the guest room at my house since no one else would be there. She refused, saying in no circumstance would she ever feel comfortable in my home. So, she and Ava stayed in a hotel near me.

One afternoon, we went to lunch with her dad and sister. I felt so out of place and exposed. Our secret was no longer a secret. The lunch started off nerve-racking on my part. Not knowing what to say, I stayed quiet. It wasn't denial or even shame. I just didn't know how Kim's family would treat me after everything.

Harold was kind and accepted our truth with no judgment. He explained why he made Kim invite me. The situation was bad, but he knew that we were still good people and wanted to make sure we didn't forget it.

Kim told her father what I went through with my wife. Harold offered his support. He also encouraged me to keep fighting for Layla. I expected their reactions to match Mrs. Duncan's behavior. It shocked me how forgiving the rest of her family was about this. They made me feel like one of them.

We planned Ava's first birthday party together with Keisha's help. I put a deposit down for a bounce house venue. We chose a theme and went to Party City together for goodie bags and things. Keisha showed us the ropes for throwing a reasonable party.

Something changed in Kim's appearance. She didn't dress different and still wore no makeup. Somehow, she wasn't the same. I had never seen her smile so much. It was beautiful. When I asked her about it in front of Keisha, her sister credited that Evan dude. Kim blushed even more, so I changed the subject.

Kim spoke of him to her dad during lunch. I didn't like it, but like she said, I was married, and my focus had to be on my daughters. Watching her struggle with Trent for so many years was difficult, so hopefully, this dude will cherish her like she deserved.

ᛈᛈᛈ

NOVEMBER SNUCK UPON US QUICKLY. It was time for Ava's first birthday. I expressed my concerns with Kim about attending the party. I didn't want our scandal to be the center of the adult conversations. She assured me that her family would be cool, but she had the same concerns about my mom.

Mom was the only person from my family invited. The remaining attendees would only be Kim's dad, siblings, and her California family. Mrs. Duncan still refused to be around me, so she voluntarily skipped her granddaughter's birthday.

Kim was right. Nobody cared. She did apologize to my mom when she greeted her. I guess she wanted to avoid the elephant if she didn't say anything.

There were about ten kids running around the bounce house room. It sounded like one hundred with all the screams and squeals. The crazy part was that all of the adults were having just as much fun. We all took our turns at the obstacle course inflatable. That thing was no joke.

The kids ran so much and so fast all over the room. Ava wore me out. Harold took over with Ava so I could catch my breath. Kim was busy with the party coordinator.

I grabbed a bottled water and sat on a bench next to Kendrick. That was the first awkward moment of the party. Kim's cousins didn't know everything, but her brother did. He must have noticed because he told me to relax. We talked about the situation briefly and then moved on to fatherhood stories.

By the end of the night, I didn't know if her family were really okay with our mess or if they were professional actors. I was insecure about it the whole time. There's no way they could be that comfortable with me around. Either way, they were pleasant.

ᛈᛈᛈ

My first Thanksgiving without my wife felt like any other day. I stayed home and ate sandwiches. Mom tried to get me to come over my grandmother's house, but I didn't want to face my relatives. They were clueless about my personal business. She only told my grandmother about Ava. I was still convinced I'd be the center of attention since Denise and Layla weren't with me.

Later that evening, Mom stopped by with enough leftovers to last me a few days. We watched Christmas movies on Hallmark and Lifetime. She was a sucker for holiday movies.

Christmas was better. I shipped gifts to Denise's dad to give to Layla and a few things for my wife. My mom accompanied me to Ms. Vivica's home for the holidays.

Mom reacted the way I did during my first visit, but this was even better with the decorations. Every room oozed Christmas time. Even the bathrooms.

Ms. Vivica and my mom hit it off immediately. Kim and I were occupied with Ava, who kept trying to redecorate the place every chance she got.

On Christmas morning, Mom and Ms. Vivica prepared breakfast with so many things to choose from. I ate some of everything. French toast, waffles, grits, eggs, bacon, sausage, and even ham. I never ate ham slices for breakfast until today. It was perfect.

We were so stuffed and relaxed that we didn't think about opening gifts until after noon. By that time, Evan stopped by. Ava left my lap and ran to him.

"Dada," she said.

Dada? I walked over to the guy and shook his hand. "What's up? I'm Brian. Ava's dad."

"Yeah, I know. It's nice to finally meet you."

Kim, who was already next to Evan, gave me a look to not take it serious.

"Brian, this is Evan."

I rolled my eyes on the inside. "Kim can't stop talking about you." They laughed. I didn't.

"Can I talk to you for a minute?" I asked Kim.

"Uh, sure."

We walked away from another man holding my baby. I wanted to snatch her from him. Ms. Vivica invited him to eat something by the time we made it into my room.

"Before you say anything, I know what this is about. She calls everyone dada. That's one of the only words she knows."

"Somehow, I find that hard to believe."

"Brian, don't trip over that. She knows you're her father."

"Does she? Or does she think that damn Calvin Klein model is her real 'dada'?"

Kim laughed in my face.

"Don't do that, Kim. I'm serious."

"Look, I understand your frustration. Evan is not taking your place. She just sees him more. She knows who you are, Brian."

"Yeah, whatever. I don't like it. You need to stop her from calling him that."

"Boy, she's one. Let her grow up a little more and then you will see."

"Naw. She'd better be calling him Mr. whatever his last name is. How long do you plan on having this dude around my daughter?"

"It's only been three months. I don't know. I like him a lot, Brian. He adores Ava. Chill out."

"I'll chill out when dude leaves. Tell him to leave now."

"Shut up and come on. Stop acting like a child."

Kim left the room first. I waited to make sure I calmed myself down. On my way out, I heard Kim tell him about my issue.

When I entered the room, the so-called doctor explained the developmental stages of children. He assured me that she would not call him that once she can grasp more of her language skills. He even proved his point by telling Ava to repeat our different names. She called everyone some version of 'dada' except for Kim. I still didn't like it.

Ava opened her gifts from all of us, even the doctor. Then he gave Kim a box with a diamond necklace from Zales. The other women gasped at her gift as he put it around her neck.

Whatever. The charm bracelet I got her from Pandora was more personal. Mom helped me pick it out. This dude didn't do anything special.

When they kissed, it hurt. I knew that it shouldn't, but it did. My feelings for Kim still existed since I had nothing to replace them with. Denise texted me this morning that she didn't want any presents from me. No "thank you" or anything nice. She told me not to send her gifts again.

While Kim moved on, I was still in the same lonely place. Granted, she allowed me to be with my daughter. Now, I had to see her with another dude in the process.

Mom pulled me to the side to make sure I didn't fall apart. She knew the truth about how I felt when it came to Kim. So, it was awkward for her too.

I didn't have high hopes that Kim would ever change her mind about us. But this felt like an official closed door to the thought of anything more.

The day improved once Evan left. I was the only "dada" in the house. Kim apologized for inviting him over. Deep down I thought she did it purposely to make me jealous, but she genuinely felt bad for how it made me feel.

Our trip ended with my mom making a new friend and me losing out. I hated seeing my daughter get excited for another man, but it revealed that I needed to get Kim out of my system. She never belonged to me and never will.

ϸϸϸ

Denise and I got nowhere. The only way I saw Layla was through my father-in-law. He still sent me videos and pictures. Denise acted like I didn't exist and sooner than later I'd have to make my presence known. She couldn't keep this up forever because I would not take it much longer.

Another quiet night was on the agenda. My phone rang

the one unique ringtone I never dreamed of hearing. My wife had called me. When I answered, no one said anything.

"Hello. Denise, are you there?"

No response. Maybe it was a butt dial. Damn.

"I'm here," she said faintly.

"Is everything okay?"

"Yes. I...My dad suggested that I check on you. He said you might hurt yourself."

What the hell was she talking about? Then I remembered her dad telling me he would get her to talk to me one way or another on a text. I guess lying was the other way.

"Some days, life is so hard to deal."

"Brian, you aren't seriously considering...you know?"

"Could you let me come and see my daughter?"

"That's not a good idea. I can't face you yet."

"You don't have to, I promise. You can have someone else bring her. I will fly there as soon as next week if you say so."

"It's too soon."

"For who? It's been seven months. I'm dying over here. I need to see Layla."

"So, you don't want to see me?" she asked. It never occurred to me that she'd want that.

"Denise, I have made my peace. You hate me for what I did. I can't blame you for it. It hurts not being a part of Layla's life while she is this young, but I know better than to expect you to ever forgive me. In my head, any day could be the day I'd get divorce papers from you."

"So, you want a divorce?"

"No, I don't. But you're not going to take me back. You hold all the cards since you have Layla. Tell me what you want me to do. I'd rather we try to work things out, but I know I messed up in the worst way."

"Yeah, you did. This time apart and my dad made me realize what we had before. Right now I can't forgive you or even look at you the same. You slept with Kim for goodness' sake. I can't even—"

"We don't have to talk about that. I am glad you called. Would you please let me see Layla?"

"I guess it's only fair. It must be hard not seeing your kids. Kids, hmph. I can't believe you have more than I do."

"It doesn't sound right, I know. I have spent a lot of time with Ava which made things a little better, but Layla means everything and I can't imagine continuing like this."

"Rewind that. What do you mean you spent a lot of time with her? Is she there with you? I thought her mother moved back to where they were."

"She did. After you wouldn't let me come around, I convinced Kim to at least let me have a relationship with one of my daughters."

"So, you've been seeing Kim?"

"Not in that way. I only visit to be with Ava. I promise. Whenever I go, I stay at her aunt's house. So, it's not just us."

"You've been sleeping in the same house with her?"

"Yes, but in separate rooms. I swear. Nothing happened since—"

"I don't like this, Brian. You being with her. I can't deal with that."

"Dee, you don't have to. I am not doing anything but being present with my daughter. As bad as it is, she is my kid too. I cannot abandon her because of who her mother is. You have to understand that."

"Well, I don't. Her mother should have thought of that. You should have too. I can't be a part of it."

"A part of what? I just want to see Layla."

"If you do, you need to make her first. She's the one who is supposed to be here. She was created between man and wife. Not a cheater and his whore."

"Hey, wait. What's all of that for? Don't say stuff like that.

Can we get on the same page? This is about me as a father. I want to be a good one, but I can't do that if you won't allow me to. The girls are my priority. They are innocent."

"So am I. You did this to yourself."

"But now you are punishing Layla for it."

"My priority is my daughter and no one else's. Until you get yours straight, we don't want to see you."

"What do you—"

She hung up the phone.

Out of all the people involved, I'd hope she'd understand me the most. Kim knew about my past as well which was why she would never keep me from Ava.

Denise lived with me for so many years and witnessed first-hand what not having my father did to me. The many conversations we'd had about it and the promises she made that I'd never be him.

The man left my mom and me like it was nothing. She would reach out to him and give him more than enough opportunities to do the right thing. Not that we weren't struggling without him financially; it was hard. Even still, she didn't ask him for money.

My mom wanted him to be there for his son. After a while, I had to tell her to stop trying. I wished he'd love me like other dads loved their sons, but he wouldn't.

He married the woman he cheated on my mom with and they had four daughters. From where I stood, he gave them everything. That man showed them something I never thought he was capable of: love.

As a man, I couldn't imagine throwing my child away like he'd done. Even with the undesirable circumstance I was in, I would not allow my children to feel how I did growing up.

It did something to a kid when they knew who their absent parent was. It did more damage to see their parent with another family while they suffered alone feeling like a piece of trash. Thrown away as if they weren't good enough to care for or to love or to even be acknowledged. Ignored and forgotten until it was their turn to be a parent. Many people cause so much damage to their children because of how they were treated during their childhood. I didn't want to be that guy.

My daughters deserved so much from me and I intended to give them the world. Not even Denise would interfere with my determination to be the best father. Everything was on me. I couldn't fault her for being unreasonable. She didn't ask for any of this, but some way I needed to get through to her. Divorce or not, both of my kids were my priority.

$$\heartsuit\heartsuit\heartsuit$$

FOUR MONTHS LATER, my fifth flight to Atlanta landed. Denise didn't know I'd been there. The trips only lasted a day. My father-in-law set up an arrangement for me to come to town. He planned to take Layla out all day claiming to give Denise a break. He'd meet me at a park for the exchange and then leave us for half the day.

I agreed to stay about an hour away from their house, then he'd drive to meet up. This way no one would recognize us. Denise's dad kept his word to help me. I couldn't thank him enough.

My father-in-law was a tough man. He retired from the Marines, and he looked the part. But he had a soft spot for the family. Theirs was intact, but he'd seen his fair share of the effects of absent fathers in children's lives. He would say "not on my watch."

I took professional pictures with Layla, and we'd gone to Chuck E. Cheese's and similar places. She loved bounce houses just like Ava. I rented a private room for an hour and let this one-year-old run wild. Both girls kept me in shape for the weekends with them.

At the end of each day with Layla, I handed her grandfather a sleeping angel. He always encouraged me to allow no one, not even his daughter, to come between Layla and me. My father-in-law respected my persistence, and I reaped the benefits every time my daughter gazed at me with a smile as big as my love for her.

Layla beamed a light that shattered the darkness surrounding me for almost a year away from her. She remembered me even though Denise snatched her from my life at such a young age. I was proud that my daughter knew her dad.

I could now buy Layla gifts to take home with her. My father-in-law would say he'd bought them. The man had a special place in heaven waiting for him when the time came. He gave me back my joy. Everything I missed was gone, but these moments made up for it.

Trying to be a good father in secret blew my mind. Dudes jumped through hoops to avoid this job, but I had to do it covertly. No social media posts or shares to my family's text group.

Baby steps, right? Layla and I took baby steps. Hers was to explore and grow. Mine headed uphill to forgiveness and reconciliation. One day we'd both make full strides in this thing called life. Unsure of where mine would settle, I kept pushing forward.

In the past year, I had both of my daughters taken away from me to each coast of the country. My wife used my picture at the shooting range. The other woman I loved started a new relationship with another man. Layla and Ava mattered more than life itself, and I became a much better father than my own.

Life taught me that I won't get everything I want, but I'd definitely have what I need. My girls.

. . .

The End

# AFTERWORD

Okay, so I know Two Lefts was crazy. Trent and Kim's relationship was drowning, then she did the unthinkable and slept with Brian. Like, really?

Now that you've read Making a Hard Right, I hope that their human mistake didn't make you hate them too much. Lol. These two were navigating through the mess they made and the waters were rough.

I wrote this series to explore forgiveness in marriage and in friendship. How much could a person take before they snapped? Or could love be enough to overcome something so awful?

Making a Hard Right was about Kim making the tough decision, yet the right one. When kids are involved in messy situations, the adults have to do whatever they can to keep the bad in check and give them all the good from it. It's so much easier said than done.

I hope you are enjoying the drama because that's exactly what this is. Feel free to leave a review for book two of the Turns in Love series. I'd love to know what you think.

Next to read...

Straightaway: No More Turns Left (Book 3 of Turns in Love Series)

Available NOW on Amazon!

# ABOUT THE AUTHOR

Renée is from the best city on the planet—Houston. She resides there with her three kids. She writes fiction based on African American characters. Renée loves creating stories with relationship drama that can easily be found in many households. She wants readers to see themselves or recognize someone they know in her characters. If she can make you laugh, gasp, think, or even cry, then her mission will be accomplished.

Connect with Renée: www.authorramoses.com
　　On Facebook www.facebook.com/authorramoses
　　On Instagram @reneeamoses
　　On Twitter @authorramoses

Listen to Same Book, 3 Time Zones: A Book Review Podcast
　　We read one book a month and post our discussion.
　　www.sb3tzreviews.com
　　On Instagram @sb3tz_reviews

For a FREE copy of Almighty Judge Diana Duncan short backstory
　　bit.ly/TILShort
　　Or a FREE copy of Truth Is
　　bit.ly/TruthIsFC

Signup for latest news, first looks, and exclusive content: bit.ly/RAMList

# ALSO BY RENÉE A. MOSES

**Turns in Love Series**
*Two Lefts, One Right*
*Making a Hard Right**
*Straightaway*
*Wishing for Her (Christmas Short)*
*Truth Is...*

**Harris Sisters Series**
*The Cost of Loving You*
*I Thought I Knew You*
*Never Stopped Loving You*
*Not Good Enough For You*

**Standalone**
*You Could Do Damage*
*When the Time is Wright (Christmas Novella)*